# SPLICE

SPLICE is a small press with a commitment to publishing unconventional, adventurous fiction and essays. For full details on titles released by Splice, and reviews of titles from other small presses, visit Splice online at ThisIsSplice.co.uk.

First published in paperback in 2019 by Splice,
54 George Street, Innerleithen EH44 6LJ.



Paperback Edition: ISBN 978-1-9161730-5-7
Ebook Edition: ISBN 978-1-9161730-6-4

Cover Design: Elena Erisheva (Lenaer), Anton Firsik,
and Wirat Suandee/Shutterstock.

# SPLICE

edited by

Daniel Davis Wood

ThisIsSplice.co.uk

# Contents

# Foreword

FOR SOME READERS, there's no greater pleasure than opening a book with the feeling of diving into a different world. For me, though, a more powerful spell is cast by prose that feels like it belongs to *this* world, only to guide the reader into altogether stranger realms. I don't mean fantasy fiction, or magical realism, or slipstream. I mean something closer to the truly Kafkaesque, in which absurd or sinisterly supernatural events are glazed with a style that strives to respect quotidian life. I mean something in which it's difficult to gauge just how close to or far from reality the fiction wants to be; I mean fiction in which *this* world is made strange, is estranged, by an affectation of language.

In 2018–2019, Splice published three collections of stories—Dana Diehl's *Our Dreams Might Align*, Michael Conley's *Flare and Falter*, and Thomas Chadwick's *Above the Fat*—each of which, in its own distinctive way, unwove the veil between reality and the irreal. Now, in this first anthology from Splice, the authors of those collections come together with new work and new affinities, each one paired up with a new author of their choice whose fictional world shares a border with their own. So Reneé Bibby, Abi Hynes, and Victoria Manifold enter the company of Splice's explorers of the ethereal, and the points of slippage between our world and others multiply in these pages...

Daniel Davis Wood
1 July 2019

Dana Diehl

# An Introduction to
# Dana Diehl

Daniel Davis Wood

DANA DIEHL caught my eye with her knack for double vision. You won't be surprised to learn that the narrator of her story 'The Boy Who Turns Into Toads' is exactly that: an attendee at the School for Insecure and Underfoot Woodland Creatures—where students all possess the uncanny ability to shapeshift into one or another forest animal—who spends his nights dissolving into "a plague of toads." The imagery of the story allows the singular to pluralise, to multiply, but Dana's prose makes something porous of the distinction between the individual and collective pronouns: "A barn owl eats one of me," says the boy, after he has become toads, "but I don't care, because there are so many of me. ... When you're human, there's only you. But when you're animal, you are many yous." So, then, how many entities are we supposed to see when the boy says, simply, "I"? Even the phrase "double vision" doesn't really encapsulate the effect: doubles double and double again like iterations of hallucinations in an acid trip.

Dana published 'The Boy Who Turns Into Toads' in the online litmag *Necessary Fiction* in 2016, and when I saw her name appear there again several months later, I knew it was time to sit up and pay attention. In her second outing, however, she was the subject of someone else's work, as the reviewer Rachel Richardson sang the praises of other stories she'd published elsewhere. I followed the trail where it led me, to yet more double vision. But this time the doubles took on other forms. In her story 'Swallowed,' Dana found a voice for a narrator of multiple identities—"we"—with two young brothers speaking in a unified voice, as if possessing a single body, from inside the stomach of a whale. In 'Once He Was a Man,' her narrator lamented the loss of a husband who had shed his human body to become, somehow, both a computerised dataset and a scattering of light particles. In 'The Mother,' Dana described the final days of an old, dying matriarch whose genes allow her to live on inside her many descendants—"dying on the daybed," she realises, "she's surrounded by herself"—and, in 'We Know More,' Dana's ethereal style caused a man afflicted with a fatal brain tumour to disintegrate, almost, so that various natural phenomena might pass through his permeable body.

Fittingly, perfectly, Dana decided to call her first collection of stories *Our Dreams Might Align*. But while reviewers have tended to focus on the significance of the word *dreams*, praising Dana's stories for their dreamlike imagery and fabular style, the more important word, thematically, is *align*. In the unpredictable world of Dana Diehl, that's what the key players do, over and over again. One person splits into many things, then the many reconstitute the one, or else the essences of different people intermingle—at the level of consciousness as often as with their bodies. Or, if not, then a narrator will look at someone else in their world and see another person altogether—a different identity will overlay the original like a photograph subjected to double exposure. The stuff of a dream might seep into reality, it's true, but the *alignment* of the elements—of the real with the dream, of one dream with another, of tangible experience with otherworldly truths—is what gives each component of a Dana Diehl story more meanings than it seems to hold when it makes its first appearance.

'The Earth Room' is no exception. This haunting, atmospheric piece of prose adopts one face to welcome the reader in, but then lets the mask slip to reveal something of darker designs. Read just the first page, or even just the first sentence, and no doubt you'll think it quaint, maybe sort of whimsical, like the sharpest of the sketches in *Our Dreams Might Align*. But read on and you'll find 'The Earth Room' subtly shifting its form—becoming many, like the amphibian boy—as it flirts with sinister forces, nightmarish visuals, and psychological horror in the vein of David Lynch or, more recently, Ari Aster. At one point, having entered a room "filled, wall to wall, with three feet of level earth," the narrator finds herself actively hoping to discover treasures in the soil: "I want to find something that isn't supposed to be here," she says. "A fairy circle. A subterranean stream bubbling to the surface. A hibernating box turtle the size of a dinner tray." These are the dreams she would pursue. But then, as she discovers, the membrane that separates dreams from nightmares is as porous as the distinction between pronouns in Dana Diehl's moral universe—and, once it has been passed through, it's impossible to look again at one's familiar world without feeling that the logic holding existence together doesn't *really* run beneath the surface of the things we see.

# The Earth Room

THERE'S AN APARTMENT IN THE CITY that's filled, wall to wall, with three feet of level earth. The first time J. takes me home with him, he teaches me to crawl through the space: slow and patient, fingers outstretched. "So you don't sink through," he explains. "Pretend you're crossing ice."

In what must have once been a bedroom, we lie on our backs with only the edges of our hands touching. There are no paintings on the walls. No photographs or mirrors. No doors. There's no furniture, not even a bed. Only earth. It's very soft and very, very quiet. The smell reminds me of freshly dug holes, of upturned stones, of dripping caves. It reminds me of childhood summers spent wrestling through the woods behind my house. Peering into groundhog holes, looking for salamanders under rotting leaves. The smell overwhelms me with a nostalgia I hadn't even realized I harbored.

"How long has this been here?" I ask J.

He tells me it was just a habit at first. On walks in the park, he'd fill his pockets with handfuls of peat moss or dirt from planters and shake them empty when he arrived home. He liked getting out of bed and feeling dirt under his bare feet. He liked the way it absorbed the roar of the city. He wanted more. He started ordering bags of planting soil. Hundreds of pounds of it, hundreds of dollars, delivered to his apartment weekly. When his neighbors questioned him, he told them he was cultivating an indoor garden. Heirloom tomato plants. Butterfly palms to clear toxins from the air.

"One time," he said, "I forgot to pay my bills for a month and didn't even notice when my electricity was shut off. I rarely cooked at home anyway, and I stopped turning on the lights long ago." All day, he said, the sun casts a moving square of light through his curtainless windows onto the dirt. At night, the streetlights brighten the rooms.

I curl my hands into claws and dig in my fingers, almost up to my wrists. I imagine how later I'll have to pick the dirt out from under my nails, how I'll carry a bit of this place across the city with me. I ask, "How much *is* there?"

J. thinks for a moment. "I did the math once. It's somewhere north of a hundred tons. You know what else weighs that much? A radio tower. A space shuttle. A railroad locomotive engine."

He props himself up on his elbow, leans over to kiss me. As we kiss, I feel myself sinking into the soil a little. The kiss deepens. The earth pulls me closer.

When the kiss ends, we both laugh and look away a little shyly. It's been a long time since a man has been shy with me. I like it.

"I guess I should go," I say. I pause to see if he'll stop me, but he doesn't. I sit up and brush myself off. When I glance back over my shoulder, I notice the impression I made in the earth. It disturbs me a little to see this hollow echo of my body. I smooth it over with my hands.

"Goodnight," I say.

In the darkness, he's quiet.

I MOVED TO THE CITY A YEAR AGO because of a boyfriend I thought I'd marry. I found a job. I found a sushi place that was better than any I'd had in my last home. I ate there often enough for the hostess to automatically bring me a cup of hot sake when I sat down, but not so often that she knew me by name. And then the boyfriend I thought I'd marry didn't want to be a boyfriend anymore. I had to find a new apartment to live in, in a new part of the city. A new sushi restaurant. A new route to work, along unfamiliar sidewalks lined with unfamiliar vendors.

During this time, I felt a hollow open up inside me. That hollow was home to something dark and squirming, something that was both me and not me. I did everything I could to ignore it. When I wasn't working, I'd take the subway to the park and walk the trails until my lungs burned. Or I'd sit on a bench and watch the street performers. My favorite was a man who'd use a hula hoop to make gigantic bubbles that would drift over the sidewalk like blind whales before getting caught in the branches of trees and bursting. It was here, at the park, that I met the man with the apartment full of earth. After a few weeks of haunting the trails and benches I started noticing him. He also seemed to spend a lot of time on a bench doing nothing at all. Another week passed, and he started to notice me, too. We began to sit on the same bench.

He told me he went by J., like an abbreviation. He was one of those men who looked both young and old at the same time. I could tell he was older than me, though I wasn't sure if it was only by a couple of years or over a decade. He often wore gray corduroys and a black peacoat. He had nice hands with delicate knuckles. I asked him to walk with me. As we strolled through the park, our shoulders raised against the cold, I felt the hollow inside myself shrink. I started to feel again like a version of myself I recognized.

THE DAY AFTER WE KISS in J.'s apartment, I wander through the city feeling dizzy. My head has become a bowl full of dirt. I go to work. I drink coffee. I type emails in an overlit cubicle. I squint into my computer screen.

In the bathroom, I roll my sleeves up to my elbows. I turn the water on hot and wait until it's steaming before I plunge in my arms. As I wash, dirt forms trails on my skin and puddles in the sink before it disappears down the drain. I try to imagine what J.'s apartment must have looked like with just an inch of earth, or a foot, or two. It's like a game I used to play as a child, when I'd drape myself upside down from the couch and try to convince myself that the ceiling was the floor, that the house as I knew it wasn't what it seemed. I imagine J.'s furniture slowly becoming submerged in earth, the rugs disappearing, then framed photographs of family, then the couch, the kitchen table. I wonder if he removed the furniture long ago, or if it was still there. I wonder if he had, *has*, a regular home buried under all that earth.

I realize I've been standing with my arms in the water for too long. My skin has blanched and wrinkled. I return to my desk to find one of my co-workers waiting for me. She asks me about a project we're working on together, asks for numbers I should remember but don't. I can't seem to focus on her face. She stops in the middle of a sentence. She tells me I should go home early. I don't look so good.

"Yeah," I say, "Maybe you're right."

I leave at barely ten in the morning. Outside the building I smell shawarma and car exhaust. I could retreat to familiar surroundings, take the subway south, bunker down in my loft above the Jamaican restaurant where, from morning to night, I can hear the chefs shouting over the sound of clinking dishes. My apartment always smells like festivals and fried plantains and the meat special of the day. I loved those smells when I first moved in, though lately they've left me disoriented. I feel like a dog in a park, losing itself in a plethora of scents. So I think of J.'s apartment. The cool earth under my palms. The simplicity of a space filled with nothing but earth. I walk north. If I change my mind, I tell myself, I can always hop on a subway or call a cab to take me home.

When J. had taken me home, last night, I'd been surprised to realize he lived in my old neighborhood, just blocks from where

I'd lived with my ex. I'd walked by his building a hundred times, never knowing that a mass of earth, of impossible weight, was suspended above me. It makes me wonder what other apartments contain. As I walk now, I imagine an apartment full of sea water, full of hornets, full of fur. I start to see the city as a world full of hidden pockets, of self-contained worlds existing inside the larger world.

I arrive at J.'s building and slip inside as someone else is leaving. I climb the stairs to the third story. A moment of doubt stops me in the hallway; I'm unsure which door belongs to him. But then I remember the windows letting in streetlight and I walk to the end of the hall: 302. I knock. No-one answers. No sound of footsteps from the other side of the door, though I remind myself there wouldn't be. I knock again. I wait.

I'm tired, so tired, and under my clothes I feel sweaty. Maybe I walked too fast, too long in the heat, or maybe I'm flushed, feverish. The thought of descending the stairs and staggering home makes me want to cry.

When I put my hand on the cool knob and turn it, the door swings outward with ease.

A three-foot wall of earth stands in front of me.

I crawl up onto the earth and pull the door closed behind me.

"Hello?" I say into the cool darkness of the apartment. But I already know the place is empty. Without doors, you can see inside every room from the entryway.

I crawl to the bedroom as J. taught me to do: slow and patient, fingers outstretched. The earth has a texture like wet moss under my palms. It reminds me of water gathering at the bottom of empty flowerpots. In the bedroom, I drop onto my side and the earth embraces me. I can already feel it cooling my body, bringing me back to normal. I sigh and close my eyes.

When I open my eyes again I find a small mushroom growing from the ground just a few inches in front of my face. It has a white dome and a pinkish stalk. I reach out and pluck it from the soil. It resists slightly, but dislodges with mycelium trailing from its end. It is light and feathery. I wonder how it'd taste, and as I wonder this I'm already placing it on my tongue. It's earthy. A little spicy. I know I should spit it out, but I feel somehow as if this moment has already been written and I already know that I will swallow the mushroom. I do. I swallow it whole. I don't even feel it moving down my throat.

I imagine the mushroom rooting itself in my belly, its mycelium traveling through my bloodstream, tendrils reaching out through all the hollow parts of me.

The earth is cool against my hot skin.

The mushroom in my belly releases spores that grow whole new mushrooms. Caps umbrella-open in my throat, between my pelvic bones.

Outside, a tree taps its branches against the window.

My body is part fungi.

I let my eyelids drop.

WHEN I WAKE, I find J. sitting cross-legged in the earth beside me. He holds a hand to my forehead.

I sit up, my tongue dry. I wipe at my mouth with the backs of my fingers, and when I pull away there's dirt on my skin. I have no idea how long I've slept. The apartment is mostly dark now, and I can see the orange glow of the streetlights coming through the windows. I'm still in my office clothes: chunky heels, slacks, a buttoned-up cardigan.

"I was sick today," I say. "I left work early. I'm sorry, I shouldn't have come here, I don't know why I did. The door was open."

In J.'s lap are two large Styrofoam containers with plastic lids. "Ramen," he says. "I went out for dinner while you were asleep. How are you feeling now?"

"Better," I say. It's true. My fever has broken. I feel so much better that part of me wonders if my sickness had been only in my head. "There was a mushroom," I say. "Before I fell asleep."

"Sometimes that happens," says J. "I always think of this as a place that never changes, but then I'll be surprised by something that crawls out of the ground."

I want to ask him if he knows what kind of mushroom it was, but then he might ask to see it and I'd have to admit I ate a mushroom I couldn't identify—ate it just because I could.

J. begins to peel the lids off the ramen. For a second, with his head dipped into the steam rising from the broth, he looks like someone else, like someone I might have dated once. For a second, my pulse quickens and I feel that hollowness under my ribcage, that familiar dark, that squirmy space, reminding me it hasn't gone away. I imagine the mycelium in my stomach twitching towards the hollowness, stretching to fill it. But the feeling passes. Now I have a warm container of ramen in my lap, and J. is smiling at me, and things are okay again.


My LAST BOYFRIEND, the boyfriend I thought I'd marry, took up a new hobby every six months or so. First, it was Dungeons and Dragons campaigns, hosted in our living room every Sunday. Then it was glassblowing. Then woodcarving. He liked me to be involved in his hobbies with him, so I was. I fought hobgoblins with my Level-2 druid spells. I blew green glass goblets to go along his blue ones. I sanded down the barely-recognizable animal figures he'd carved with his Swiss Army knife.

When we moved to the city, he signed us up for pottery classes. Everything I made came out of the kiln feeling impossibly heavy.

Bowls made for Vikings. Mugs made for giants. He used the bowls and mugs anyway, despite their impracticality. The first time I saw him sipping coffee from something I'd made, I thought he was trying to be funny. He wasn't. He really liked my mugs. I added that to the list of reasons we should be together. I had a running list I kept without really trying to. Anyway, pottery was probably his favorite of all the hobbies he ever spent time on. He was still doing it when we broke up, filling our then-shared apartment with vases and bowls and plates the size of frisbees. He said he liked that we were making art out of a raw material that had taken thousands of years to form. Some clay deposits had been hidden underground for millennia before someone stumbled upon them. "Nothing can hide underground forever," he told me. "Eventually everything finds its way to the surface."

AFTER DINNER, J. asks me to spend the night.

I start to shake my head, and he says, "No pressure. But you're sick. You should rest."

I think about refusing, but he's right. Although my fever has broken, my apartment feels as if it's a whole country away. Just imagining the miles of underground tunnels separating me from my bed makes me tired.

I lie on my side, facing J. He lies next to me, looking up at the ceiling, a respectful space between us. In the other room, the walls change from green to yellow to red.

"I remember the sickest I've ever been," J. says suddenly. "I was seven or eight. It was nighttime, and I was alone in my bedroom. All I could see was a sliver of light under my door. My parents were in the living room, watching television, but I couldn't call to them, no matter how hard I tried. I kept hallucinating that one of them would come to my door and I'd ask for water, but then they'd leave and the hallucination would start all over again."

This is the first time he's told me anything about his past. I want to ask where he grew up. Where his parents were now. How many girls he's brought back to this apartment. How many people, other than me, know about this space full of earth. But before I can do that, he's asleep, snoring lightly. The sound is soft and pleasant, like wind moving through a tunnel. I watch him in the artificial light, looking for that shapeshifting quality I'd seen earlier in his face, but this time he just looks like himself.

As I wait for sleep to descend on me, I can't help thinking of what he said earlier—about things that grow up out of his floor and surprise him. A piece of information dislodges from my brain. A handful of soil contains between one hundred and one thousand antropods, smaller than the eye can see, and up to fifty billion bacteria. I imagine all the invisible worlds teeming under our feet, transforming and evolving as we eat, as we sleep, as we brush skin, as we kiss. Every now and then something grows big enough to break the surface.

I want to find something. I want to find something that isn't supposed to be here. A fairy circle. A subterranean stream bubbling to the surface. A hibernating box turtle the size of a dinner tray.

I roll onto my hands and knees and crawl into the living area. I go to the windows, thinking that this is where things are most likely to grow, fed by sunlight and the artificial colors of the city. I bring my face close to the earth. It's musky, sweet, and smooth.

I start to dig. I dig with my fingers, push dirt out of the way with my arms, my elbows. I wonder if I could keep digging to reach the first dirt. Dirt he dropped here years ago, during a different time in his life.

I'm nearly a foot down when my fingers scrape against something hard. I reach in deeper and close my fist around it and pull it loose from the ground. I open my hand to find a twenty-sided die, still caked in dirt, resting in my palm. I stare at it. It's emerald, with white numbers, like something I used to play with, something I'd been persuaded to play with. The edges are dulled and rounded down. It's been well-used.

I shake my head.

I drop the die back into the hole, but I don't bury it. I leave the hole as it is. I crawl back into the bedroom and lay down in the hollow my body made before I left.

J. talks in his sleep. "Who was he?" he mumbles. "He's here." He gasps.

I pick the dirt out from underneath my fingernails. I wait for J.'s breathing to return to normal.

I leave at dawn, so I have enough time to return to my own apartment and change before heading into work.

All morning at my desk, I think of the hole I dug in the apartment, the hole containing the die. I have this feeling that if I'd kept digging, I would have found more. I both want to and don't want to see what else the earth contains. I try to throw myself into my work, but I can't focus on what I'm supposed to be doing. My arms feel electric, as though the mushroom's mycelium have wormed into my muscles and are fighting to take control of me. I close my eyes and rest my face in my palms. In my mind, I'm tunneling through J.'s apartment. My cells have been digested by the mushroom and transformed into earth. My body belongs to the ground. I decide I'll go back. I tell myself I'm just confused about what I found. All I need to do is see the apartment in the light of day, to know everything is okay. As soon as I've made this decision, I feel better.

I leave the office at noon. J. was gone around lunchtime yesterday. I guess maybe he'll be gone again today, too. When I reach his apartment, the door is unlocked. This doesn't make me suspicious. Why lock your door when all your home contains is earth? But if J. shows up before I can leave, I wonder: what would I say?

That I forgot something? That I left something behind? I unlatch my watch from around my wrist and fling it across the room: it's an excuse as good as any. Then I return to the hole I'd dug in the night. It's undisturbed. I reach in and find the twenty-sided die. It's warm, as if it has spent the day clutched in someone's sweaty palm. I place it on the earth next to me, then I take off my work jacket so it doesn't get dirty, I roll up the hem of my dress past my knees, and I kneel in the dirt by the hole and dig down further than before.

It's such a relief to be digging. I love the feeling of loose earth in my hands. I love the changes in smell and color the deeper I dig. Before long, I've found something else. I blow off the dirt. A Swiss Army knife. I place it next to the dice. I keep digging. Next, I find a blue glass goblet. I wipe the dirt off the rim with my thumb. My hands are shaking.

Did J. leave these items here for me? Or did they leave themselves? Did these things I'd been trying to leave behind follow me here?

I feel like I'm getting close to the bottom. Now I have to lie flat on my stomach to reach in and continue scraping up the soil. Part of me wants to run away, but another part of me has to keep going. What will happen when I reach the floor?

Before I can find out, I hear the door close behind me.

I turn. J. is on his knees, watching me.

Except it's not J. Or it is J., but he's also someone else. It's like when you're walking through an airport, and you think you recognize someone you know, someone close to you, like your brother, and you're sure it's him, but then you see the stranger from a different angle and it's clearly not him, and you have no idea how you confused him for someone else in the first place.

The man in front of me is J.

The man is also my ex.

He has my ex's dark eyebrows and deep-set eyes. But he has J.'s downturned mouth and J.'s long eyelashes. And as I look more closely, I realize he doesn't just look like my ex; he looks like every boy I've ever loved, or liked enough to sleep with.

"Who am I?" he says.

I wait for that hollow to widen inside me. To fill me with terror. I expect it to get so wide I'll feel it taut under my skin. But I don't. I feel solid. I feel heavy.

I reach out and take his hand.

"It's okay," I say.

We lower ourselves into the hole I've dug. Together, inside, we continue to dig. We find more things. A class ring I wore only once. A state champion tennis medal. A beaded bracelet I recognize from my tenth birthday. A chipped water glass. Other objects, objects I don't recognize, objects from someone else's life. We dig. After a while, the earth starts to collapse back in on us, burying our legs, our waists, our chests. And we don't push it away. We let ourselves join the snaking strands of mycelium, the earthworms, the small creatures that have not yet woken up.

*from*

# The Sanctuary

SATURDAY IS ABORTION DAY AT Happy Bellies: Potbelly Pig Rescue and Sanctuary.

I used to be upset by this, the idea of all those potential somethings becoming nothings, but a lot of things that used to upset me don't upset me anymore.

I see the veterinarian coming from miles away, a smudge of brown dust to the west. He's late, probably got lost on the winding backroads that lead from here to the interstate. I wipe sweat off my upper lip with the back of my hand and lock up the pen where I've spent all morning lathering sunscreen onto the pigs' backs and the tips of their ears. I pull my Happy Bellies baseball cap down over my forehead. Nine o'clock and already the heat blisters across the desert. The world flattens under its weight.

I reach the parking lot at the same time as the vet. I can tell he's never been here before by the way he carefully maneuvers around the potholes and doesn't know to park in the shade of the mesquite tree. It'll be over a hundred and thirty degrees in his car by the time he leaves.

"It's beautiful out here," he says, shielding his eyes as he steps out of the car.

That's what everyone says the first time they see the desert. And although it's true that it's beautiful, I've learned that what they really mean is, Why would anyone choose this place to build a Pig Sanctuary? When it monsoons, flash floods muscle over the washes and onto the roads, trapping the staff on an island of pigs. In the hottest months we have to drive an hour south to Tucson twice a day, sometimes three times, to stock up on potable water. We can drain two thousand gallons in under twelve hours. In July and August, we chill towers of wet towels in our industrial-sized freezers and drape them over the pigs' backs so nobody overheats.

"Thomas," he says, extending his hand.

His fingers envelop mine. He's tall enough that I have to squint up at his face and cup my eyes with my free hand. He's much younger than the last vet who came out here to work with us, but he's still older than me. He has thick eyebrows and brown eyes and shoulder-length hair tucked behind his ears. But the most noticeable thing about him is his mouth. It seems too big for his face, drooping down at the corners like it's trying to slide off.

I release his hand.

"You can set up in here," I say, and show him into the small ranch house that we've repurposed into a visitor center and clinic. He rolls a large, black case behind him. It makes me think of a magician's kit. I try not to stare at it, wondering what it might contain.

"Sorry about all this," I say, waving at the boxes of souvenir T-shirts and outdated pig-themed calendars and piles of neatly folded comforters donated by guests for when the weather turns cold. "The clinic space is in the back."

I leave him flipping through a box of potbelly pig magnets as I go to fetch one of my favorite pigs from her pen. Lucy. We noticed the drag in her belly a few days ago. Most of the pigs we need to perform abortions on are new to the Sanctuary. Before we introduce a pig to the others, we always make sure they are spayed or neutered. But we've had Lucy for a few weeks now. Somehow she must have slipped through the cracks in the system, such as it is.

Lucy smells like maple syrup. Petting her is like petting a hairy boulder. A single fang protrudes from under her top lip. Her eyes are almost completely hidden under rolls of forehead fat. Her neck wobbles as she hoofs toward me. Lucy is my favorite, because I am her favorite. She's possibly the ugliest pig in our care, but she doesn't seem to know it. She's the quickest to roll onto her back for a belly rub, and when I'm doing my rounds she'll follow me at my heels like a puppy.

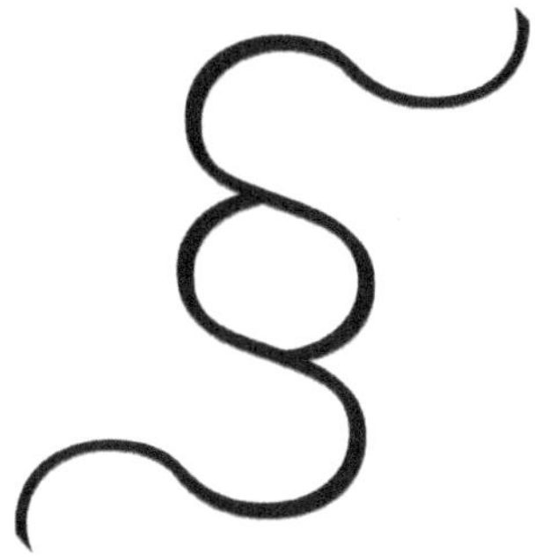

Dana Diehl's 'The Sanctuary'
is available in its entirety at
ThisIsSplice.co.uk/2018/04/16/the-sanctuary

Reneé Bibby

# An Introduction to
# Reneé Bibby

Dana Diehl

I FIRST MET RENEÉ BIBBY at Cartel Coffee Lab in downtown Tucson, Arizona, in late 2015. I was new to the area, fresh out of my MFA, and yet to find my place in the writing community in this strange, beautiful desert city. A friend told me about Reneé and assured me she'd welcome me with open arms. Which is exactly what happened. Reneé is warm and enthusiastic, and has a talent for fostering communities and making everyone feel included. She is the Director of The Writers Studios in Tucson, where she teaches beginning and advanced classes. She is also the organizer of an informal, weekly writing group called Write Wednesday, where local writers meet up for a few hours each week to work together.

The first story of hers that I read was a very short piece called 'Rabbit or the Wheel,' published online in *Wildness*. It's a sketch about a man at a bus station, awaiting a sister who doesn't show up. On his way back home, driving through the desert alone, the man runs over a rabbit. I remember being startled by the quiet, innocuous way that Reneé allows violence to enter into the story:

"There is the wild brief flash of white paws, and then the rabbit goes silently under his wheel." The man doesn't run over the rabbit; the rabbit "goes"—*silently*—"under." In this one brilliant sentence, Reneé unexpectedly shifts the agency away from the driver and onto the animal. Then, when the man realizes he has hit something, he stops and exits the car to investigate, and Reneé pulls another trick. Turning the reader away from the obvious—away from the carnage the man must see—she points instead to the prickly pear at the edge of the road, its fruit "swell[ing] blood, freckled and white." So she shows us the dead rabbit by *not* showing us the dead rabbit, by giving us the red of blood and the white of bone in an image of swollen fruit, close to bursting, so that what we see is even more horrifying than the roadkill.

Reneé's work is full of magic like this. She directs her reader's attention towards what is on the sidelines of perception. She shows us what escapes our notice, what "goes silently under" our ordinary habits of vision, what we wouldn't think to look at on our own. Her characters are people who do what they're supposed to do—pay their bills, mark their calendars, keep their heads down at work—until an event cracks them out of their complacency, splits them open like an animal on the asphalt.

In the story you're about to read, Reneé depicts the dilemmas of a man whose hair has started talking. The man, Kingston, is black, and has a way of keeping himself to himself in order to get ahead in the workplace. But his hair is more outspoken than he is, more charismatic, less afraid to voice its opinion—and it even resents his inertia, the way he has sacrificed his ambition to avoid unsettling his white co-workers. "A black man shouldn't give up something to get on," it warns him at the end of the story, and, together with the criticisms of his wife (who takes the side of the talking hair), the interventions of the hair force Kingston to look back at his lifelong tendency to hold his tongue, to voluntarily shrink his own horizons. The incident forces this man to confront the ways in which he has been suppressing his own blackness out of deference to a white culture, out of fear of what the world will see in him, and his trouble is both hilarious and heart-wrenching. Just as Reneé Bibby brings warmth and empathy to her writing communities, she also approaches her characters with a generous heart, a sense of curiosity, a sharp eye, and an infectious passion for the world—and the evidence for that can be found right here.

# That Boy

Grown out from a close shave, Kingston's hair spoke to the woman beside him on the number six bus: tiny, high-pitched voices in unison admired the boldness of the flowers on her blouse. Kingston thought, *Not this old rigmarole.* The woman grinned up at his hair, which was long enough now to start coiling in a slight poof, and started a story about finding the blouse with the tags still on it at the Goodwill half-price sale, and kept talking even as Kingston tried to read the *Times.*

At work, Kingston went straight to the bathroom to look at his hair in the mirror. He told it to behave. His hair made no promises.

Kingston liked his job. Upper management asked for his input, sometimes took his advice. His direct reports gave him positive ratings on semi-annual reviews. He watched the network TV shows and kept up with sports, so he had material for chats in the breakroom. He played weekend golf well enough to keep up on the occasional outing, but not so well as to be taken as ambitious. He bought Girl Scout cookies and overpriced wrapping paper for his coworkers' kids' fundraisers. If someone asked him a question, he usually knew the answer.

*We are two years away from retirement; we have a good setup,* he thought to his hair at the meeting. *Do not rock the boat. Do not.*

"Anything else about third-quarter projections?" asked Jim.

"Given the yearly return margins, we should invest in flexible work schedules for staff," said Kingston's hair.

Jim glanced at the hair, then at Kingston's face. "What was that?"

*Do* not *share private conversations I've had with others!*

Kingston's hair went on ahead: "Marsha in accounting has run some preliminary numbers and it seems feasible to implement without a loss of productivity."

All eyes swiveled to Marsha. "Well," she said, "it—it does."

"Kingston's... *hair?*" Jim said. "What's this about?"

No way Kingston would let his hair take over. "My staff," he said in a rush so fast it was almost a splutter, "my staff have been asking about more flexibility. Some of them drive down from Vancouver and that's an hour's commute. They have kids to pick up, and sometimes parents to take care of. We've seen lower than usual satisfaction numbers on the staff survey, so I had Marsha run some numbers. Some preliminary data—"

"The Stanford work survey," his hair interjected.

"—has indicated a higher level of employee output in flexible schedule setups. We could test a pilot group with some options."

Other managers murmured support for the project. Jim surveyed the room before arriving at a decision. "Well, then, Marsha," he said. "Get me the numbers. We'll take a look and get back to you."

In the bathroom, Kingston threatened to shave his head if his hair ever spoke out at a meeting again.

"Hey," his hair argued back, "you couldn't have asked for a better opening to pitch the idea!"

"That wasn't a pitch meeting. That's not the order of operations! I had a meeting set up with Ron and he—"

"Ron? That joker? Nah, he'll steal all the credit."

"So what? If that's what it takes to get the program up and running."

"Why are you hiding behind Ron?"

"I'm not hiding! I don't have an ego that needs feeding. My way is *smart.* Political. Understanding how to work a system for optimal outcomes."

"You mean, it's making sure the idea has a white person pushing it forward."

Kingston saw his own look of rage in the bathroom mirror and wondered if it were powerful enough to sear the hair off his head. He said, "This is *not* about race."

A toilet flushed and Matt DiGorgi clanged out of one of the stalls. He was a potato-shaped Accounts Payable intern with a thicket of overgrown curls an unfortunate shade of Ronald McDonald red. He edged towards the adjacent sink with an apologetic glance at Kingston and hunched to wash his freckled hands with an epidemiologist's ideal amount of soap and time, murmuring, "Sorry, sorry, just, ah, a second," all the while. At the towel dispenser the cheap feed jammed. Flushed and sweating, Matt rammed big fingers into the gap to eke out a few strips of paper. He dared to look into Kingston's eyes in the mirror. He gestured to his own curls, "Hair, ammirite?"

"Get the hell out of here, man!" the hair hollered.

Matt scuttled away, trailing apologies after him: "Sorry, yes, right, *sorry!*"

"You're fooling yourself if you don't know that everything is about race," said the hair.

Kingston pointed at his hair. "I'm picking up fresh razors on my way home."

At home his wife, Katayounn, watched him tear open a packet of razors at the bathroom sink.

"Kingy," she said, "why aren't you using your electric shaver?"

"Katy," his hair yelled, "put something sad on the record player so he can melodramatically shave us with cheap razors."

Katayounn *tsk*ed and ran her hand over the curve of Kingston's head, using the edge of her thumb to tame a cowlick. "Didn't you say you were too old to be bald anymore?" she said.

That was true; time had thinned Kingston's face into severe cheekbones and forehead, and the curlicues of gray softened his aspect. It's why he'd forgone the shave a few days back. The memory of his somewhat asymmetrical pate glowing like a lamp in their holiday studio photos had been enough to prompt him to risk the chance his hair might talk.

"You'd be okay if I grew a giant afro?"

"Yes, she would," his hair insisted.

If she'd answered right away, he wouldn't have believed her, but she considered him in the mirror. "You're nearly bald for real in the front, Kingy. I don't think it's something you can pull off."

"That's not what I mean. I don't want to grow an afro."

"We would look *so good* if you did," his hair said.

"I mean, would you like me if I had an afro?"

"*Like* you?" said Katayounn.

"Yeah, would we be together if I had an afro?"

"Who do you think I am? Like I wouldn't be with you if you had different hair? Do you think you could change something so superficial and destroy our marriage? Like, if I came home with blonde hair one day you'd reconsider our entire relationship?"

Kingston turned to look at her directly. "You and blonde hair is different. You looking like a bleach blonde is not the same as *black* hair. You're not American; maybe you don't understand—"

"Oh no!" his hair squeaked.

Katayounn had a stone cold look, a you're-getting-close-to-my-last-nerve look, and she leveled it at him, the mile warning gunshot on the track of the conversation. "I'm sorry," she said, "but did you forget, *I'm* not white, either. I grew up here. Raised kids who are part black so don't—"

"But you're not *black*," he said suddenly. Before she could take umbrage, he cut in and undercut himself: "Maybe I'm not black, either."

His hair chimed in, stridently. "Don't say that. Don't deny who you are. You *are* black."

"Kingston, you look black. It's not just the hair."

Kingston felt dangerously close to tears with the two of them coming at him. "I *know*—I have black skin, but what I mean is what if I don't *act* black. Katy, just admit—admit that if I'd shown up as a young buck with a big ass afro your parents would not have approved of us getting married."

He'd reached the end of her forbearance. "*Your* mom would never have approved."

When Kingston was seven, his hair sassed his mom about cleaning his room and quick as a ninja she had had him by the collar, "Nuh-uh, we are *not* doing this," dragging him to the car—his white father watching them, wide-eyed, as they swept through the living room—to drive him straight to the barber. Arms folded, she'd stood behind the barber and insisted: "We're not having this, Kingston James. You're not going to be *that* boy."

He didn't know who *that* boy was. Much later, after they moved to Atlanta his junior year of high school, he met the street-smart black teens with dreads, braids, fades, meticulous edges, and intricately shaved hair patterns, recognized them, one and all, as manifestations of the boy his mother feared he'd become: confident, loud code-talkers crowding the high school hallways, with their wild-patterned clothes and low-slung jeans visibly rejecting the parameters of success that were, he realized much later, inextricably linked to whiteness.

But before he could get to public high school and understand that his mother's ideas were based on real people, *that* boy haunted him, a boy-shaped shadow awaiting the cover of night to creep into his bed—to use his hair to infect him, to somehow warp his humanity into a simulacrum, to transform him into an almost-boy for his family to be ashamed of. But his mother had saved him by divesting him of the dangerous lure of his hair, the tantalizing growing thickness that would draw *that* boy in. Kingston's fear of the specter of *that* boy was so intense he couldn't ask his trusted father about it, for later at dinner when his dad offered him a tender look, rubbed his bare head, gave it a quick kiss, Kingston took all this to mean that his father was as relieved as his mom to have the threat disarmed.

He conceded the point to Katayounn. "My mom wouldn't have liked my hair."

Katayounn could level a loving look as quick as an angry one. She rubbed his head again, thumbing whorls of his hair as if he were a baby kitten. "So, then," she said. "What do you want to do with your hair?"

Kingston studied his reflection. His hair grew in slightly patchworked coils of gray.

"Don't be ashamed of us," his hair said.

"I'm not ashamed," he insisted. But he was ashamed. So deeply and intensely that in everyday conversation with a klatch of white people something would catch his eyes—maybe their bare, neon white legs in a row, maybe the floral-printed pastel hems of a bunch of cardigans—and he'd become very aware of his own obvious one-of-these-is-not-like-the-others that shame and awkwardness would choke him up and constrict the words he was trying to say. It had been this way for him ever since the barber, that cigar-chewing, beefy slab of a man, pushed his head down with a rough hand to buzz up the back of his head. It had been, for him, a lifetime of living with this sense that something fundamental in his existence, something that he could not uproot, was *dirty*, was chum in the water for the creature of a whole other type of man. He'd have to bow out of conversations, gather himself together in private, remind himself in bathroom stalls: "You a college-educated veteran, married to a woman with a PhD. You know how to golf, it's not just for white people. Look at Tiger Woods."

His hair knew this, of course, and called him on it. Unshelled him right there in the bathroom with Katayounn. Kingston couldn't name the feeling that overcame him in that moment, a molten upwelling that caused his breath to stutter. Part of it was shame, an accretion of shame, layers built up over time, all the times at lacrosse meets when the other parents asked his dad if Kingston was adopted, all the times the black boys in the hall had chanted *coconut!* while pelting him with footballs, all the times he'd noticed passing women adjusting their purses, and now the fresh scratch of Katayounn in the room to witnessing his new disarmament—but also grief, rising and burning through the scars of his shame.

Katayounn squeezed his arm. "I like it, Kingy. I like the hair. It makes you look presidential."

His hair grew over the next month. It grew chattier and more ebullient, the tiny voices talking amongst themselves. It loved the bus. The sleepy men on their way home from night shift, the old ladies clutching folders of social security and welfare papers, the gaggle of oblivious teenagers bumping people with their school backpacks, the disheveled homeless men generating a miasma of stay-away in the back seats. He'd always loved the bus ride for the quiet, for the chance of a leisurely read on his way to work, but now his hair chatted to them all, whipping up a whirl of constant conversation, asking after kids, work, weather, updates on other passengers. Kingston pretended to read, but his hair shared personal anecdotes about Katayounn, about his kids, and so he bookmarked his place with a thumb, folded over his paper to join in the conversation, did his best to moderate his hair's embellishments of the truth. Left unchecked his hair would have his daughter heralded as the youngest-ever United Nations ambassador, his son a millionaire dentist, and Katayounn a Nobel Prize-winning researcher. So he became known to them, the other passengers, and over the course of the month they, too, became more familiar to him. By the end of the week the bus driver would pick him up with a lively swing of the door and a joyous greeting: "Kingston! My main man!" "La'Terre!" his hair would respond and Kingston would slap-shake the driver's hand—"How you been?"—and take part in a ritual he'd always taken pains to avoid, feeling too stiff to have ever pulled off with ease.

At work it wasn't so simple to see how his hair fit in. Ron, his boss, kept his eyes on Kingston's face but talked in a new way, overly jovial, which seemed to be more about the hair. For its part, his hair was having none of it, keeping cool with long silences and monosyllables, withholding that little shred of approval Ron seemed so desperate to receive. Kingston's own effusiveness did nothing to offset Ron's growing anxiety in conversation, and once Ron had exhausted all his jokes and questions about the weekend the hair would coolly cut him off.

"What about that pilot project proposal we submitted?" asked the hair.

"Yep, that's right!" Ron beamed. "Taking all your reports to Jim. Will get you some feedback. Preliminarily: we like it. Think it's a cool idea."

Hunter, a young white guy from Engineering, heard Kingston's hair talking in the breakroom and pushed Janet from Payroll out of the way to get near.

"This is freaking magnificent!"

"Who's this guy?" Kingston's hair asked.

"I'm Hunter! From Engineering! I'm just... *wow*. Kingston's *hair*. Nice to meet you."

The air in the breakroom grew tense as people tuned into the conversation.

Kingston's hair said, "Okay, white dude, slow your roll."

"Ha! Did you hear that?" Hunter polled the room. "It called me 'white dude.' I am, I *am* a white dude."

Kingston kept stirring creamer into his coffee. *I've never called anybody 'white dude' in my life!* he thought. *What are you playing at here, hair?*

But even the hair seemed confused. It asked Hunter: "Why are you so excited about that?"

"Because at last we can talk. You know, about real shit."

"Real shit?"

Kingston sipped his coffee, staying out of it.

"Yeah! Let's talk about race stuff. Real shit."

Gasps and a few titters erupted from the assembled.

Hunter polled the room again. "What? Am I supposed to pretend he's not black? We supposed to be 'color blind' and shit?"

People pointedly looked away, as if the answer was yes, yes indeed, they were supposed to pretend he wasn't any different than them. The only other black person in the breakroom was Stacey from Sales. She kept her eyes on the exchange, tapping a spoon on her upper lip while the microwave whirred behind her and nuked her lunch. The collective reprobation instantly turned Kingston's hair's opinion in favor of Hunter.

"Okay, have some coffee with us, Hunter from Engineering," the hair suggested. Kingston was sitting at a round Formica table strewn with half-read newspapers and tickets to a local improv show. Hunter bobbed delightedly into the chair beside him and then, after the microwaved dinged, Stacey brought her lunch to the table too.

"This is gonna be good," she said.

But Hunter skipped a lot of the warm-up questions about hair texture and liking fried chicken and asked instead about Kingston's life: prep schools, summer math camps, trips abroad. Hunter had grown up poor in Detroit, biking in the streets in a pack of black boys, and Stacey had grown up in San Francisco, aspiring to be a Broadway star before her dad's cancer had called her home from art school. Hunter teased Stacey and she teased back and all of them laughed so loudly they could be heard down the hall.

At the end of his lunch hour Kingston left the breakroom smiling, looking backwards at Hunter and Stacey still cackling, and nearly knocked over Jill Young. A birdlike woman from Accounting who flitted about the office in bright floral outfits with super-shiny ballet flats and old man cardigans to fight off the relentless air conditioning, Jill felt delicate and crushable as Kingston's bulk collided with her. He grabbed her upper arms to steady them both, pausing long enough to verify they'd each found their footing again. Jill meeped and blinked giant blue eyes at Kingston like an owlet.

He started, "So sorry—" but in the rush of adrenaline he couldn't recall her name, so he said, lamely, "little lady, didn't mean walk into you."

Jill gripped files tighter to her chest and kept blinking.

Kingston's hair said, "You okay?"

Jill nodded, stepped around Kingston, and flew down the hall.

Later that day, Jim, the CEO, knocked on Kingston's open door and slid right into a spare seat at Kingston's desk while asking, "Hey, you got a minute?" He looked Kingston directly in the eye, not at his hair, and said, "Listen, we're not going to proceed with the work from home pilot. Numbers look good on paper, but I ran it by some other managers and they're not keen to have their staff out of sight."

Many things filtered through Kingston's mind, about bad supervisors, trusting teams, and the biased polling of supervisors. He couldn't have said in that moment if he wanted his hair to bust out with a rebuttal or stay quiet. His hair said nothing, cryptically mute.

"Well," Kingston said, "did we consider the programs—"

"Yeah, we looked at it from every angle. I'm afraid it's not for us." Jim rapped his knuckles on Kingston's desk. "But, hey, gotta swing and miss a few before hitting a home run, right?" In a flash he rose from his seat and moved to the door, then paused there to turn back to Kingston momentarily. "Oh, hey," he said, offhand, almost as an afterthought, "don't worry too much about that thing with Jill. Our HR gal is great; she'll get it ironed out."

"What thing with Jill?"

"Little tussle from earlier today. Just be more careful in the halls—at least until this MeToo stuff settles down, right? Okay, thanks for your work." Those last words he spoke over his shoulder as he disappeared from the doorframe like a vaudeville performer pulled offstage.

Kingston saw his reflection in the computer screen.

"Hair," he said, "what was that?"

"We don't know."

"Did the idea get rejected because it was a bad idea or because it came from the only black man on senior leadership?"

"We don't know."

"And Jill? Is it because I'm a black man? Or just a man?"

"WE DON'T KNOW."

The dark monitor reflected back his mute, shadow self, his hair a fuzzy line at the top amidst blobs of glaring fluorescents and looming dark faux-wood paneling. He couldn't bear to be there anymore. He blindly gathered papers into his briefcase and hustled out of the office without saying goodbye to anyone, sneaking past Heather, his team's receptionist, when she ducked beneath the desk to retrieve some files.

The work day hadn't ended, so he boarded a nearly empty bus. Enough room that each passenger sat alone, pressed to windows and studiously avoiding eye contact, so that even if his hair had been chatty it would have been rude, incongruous, to settle next to anyone and strike up a conversation. He went down the rows almost to the back to settle himself in a seat, solo.

Yet as the bus chugged away from the curb, he discovered he hadn't escaped himself. Someone had shined the windows so neatly that the low sun bouncing against the prism of windows and the reflective steel of buildings projected his face onto the glass. The crisscrossing interplay of light, movement, and glass created not just one version of himself, but other reflections offset and cool-toned, connected, shadowy Kingstons, who merged and pulled apart as the bus moved through the canyons of buildings.

Letting his hair grow out hadn't turned him into *that* boy— into *that* man, the type of thug his mother feared. But he'd grown into a certain type of man who wasn't afraid of that boy. A man who thought he'd gained all the benefits of those boys: socially savvy, seeing through people, understanding their real wants and needs—*having their number,* and in having their number, nobody could ever have his.

Maybe it had all been bravado? An imposter confidence. Maybe, not just him and his hair, but all those boys, years ago.

"A black man shouldn't give up something to get on," his hair insisted.

More bravado, a desperate puff of courage; Kingston didn't have the heart to argue. He let the bus rock him gently and watched his own face and his hair become dappled and bright in the backdrop of the city passing outside the window.

"Please," his hair said at last, quietly, "don't cut us."

Kingston propped his briefcase on his lap, planted his elbows on the edge and covered as much of his hair as could with the span of his fingers and palms to give it some small comfort.

Gripping harder, head bent, Kingston said, "I won't."

# *from*
# Skills in the
# Domestic Arts

YOU ARE A MOTHER at the threshold of your oldest daughter's room. You've been afraid to look, left it unchecked, and you are astounded, maybe even somewhat *impressed* by the carnage. Her space is a fresco by a master, *Explosion of Teenage Life in Modern Times:* sports bras rimmed with lines of salt dangle off her door handles; jeans, underwear, and T-shirts crumple on the floor, drape themselves over the headboard and desk chair, dribble out of the closet; balled socks are everywhere daubs of white; Lip Smackers chap sticks (Ice Cream Cake, Mango, Cherry, Cotton Candy, Peppermint, Root Beer Float) intermingle with open, half-used Blistex tins; electric blue eyeshadow kits, Great Lash mascara tubes of every shade, Wet 'N' wild polish and cotton balls speckled with color (blue, metallic black, and more blue), half-used makeup sponges, and hairbrushes clogged with wily strands obscure the top of the vanity; and then, around the periphery of the room: cleats, shin guards, sweat-slicked uniforms, running shoes, a much-loved pair of Doc Martens, flats, sandals; silver flecks of bubblegum foil and Snickers snack-size candy wrappers, old mugs clung to by dried teabags, ring pops, half-eaten sandwiches, glasses rimmed with milk or juice; the carpet layered with crumpled notes, dented sheets of old homework, pen lids, uncapped markers, and a smattering of Post-it notes with hand-drawn emojis; the décor a mishmash of candle wax, seashells layered with dust, peeling stickers (a Lisa Frank Unicorn, Pacman, Blue Ghost, Pink Ghost) on the closet door, crystalline perfume bottles with candy-colored liquid, a ratty old stuffed teddy bear and a squirrel, a knocked-over dead fern spilling its dirt, a smattering of coins, a very old Little Mermaid comforter disgorging its innards, discarded dollar bills, a leaking plastic snow globe, Mardi Gras beads in green, purple, and yellow, sticky-tack daubing the walls, plus posters (Megan Rapinoe, Billie Eilish, BTS) and newspaper articles about her sporting victories yellowed and curling off the walls. And somewhere unseen but smellable, damp towels molding into an aqueous funk.

You hadn't looked in for a while—you didn't know it'd gotten this bad. When you were young, vacuuming your bedroom curtains under supervision, first thing on a Saturday, you vowed to not become your mother. You wouldn't wake up your girls (before sons) to clean imagined dirt—clean away the *idea* of dirt. Your own children would have a space in the house wholly their own. A bedroom, a parcel of land inside the kingdom of the household, over which they would have dominion, to manage and secret away their childish lives from the inspection of adults.

Now, at the threshold of your oldest daughter's room, the sign on the door, *KEEP OUT,* is a reminder that to annex her room back into the kingdom would be a betrayal to the younger version of yourself, the furiously vacuuming girl who hadn't been allowed to choose *if* she'd clean curtains, much less dictate *when* they were vacuumed. It doesn't matter that you've opened the door because the smell had assaulted you in the hall, a sour organic interplay of ripe food, molding, and synthetic flower fragrance: you can't renege on your promise to them: *you can keep your room any way you like.*

So, you close the door and go back to our own room. They're watching TV downstairs, your husband, oldest daughter, and the youngest daughter. Your own room isn't perfect, not a study in meticulousness—you have some neatly piled clothes not put away; you can tolerate a few bottles on the vanity. Your own room is a Wyeth painting: clean lines, spare but warm-toned and calm. You can live with the oldest daughter's room. Surely.

Almost out of sight, just on the periphery of your attention, you see movement. You're not afraid of bugs. You'll pluck a spider right from the wall with bare hands and carry it outside. You don't scare easily.

You watch the cheap Sunny Health & Fitness rowing machine, unused for months and relegated to the corner of the room, move. It moves slow as a sloth, the long arm of the paddle swinging out first, the surprisingly prehensile seat and column undulating like an inch worm. You watch it creep towards the bed.

"Hey," you say, "what're you doing?"

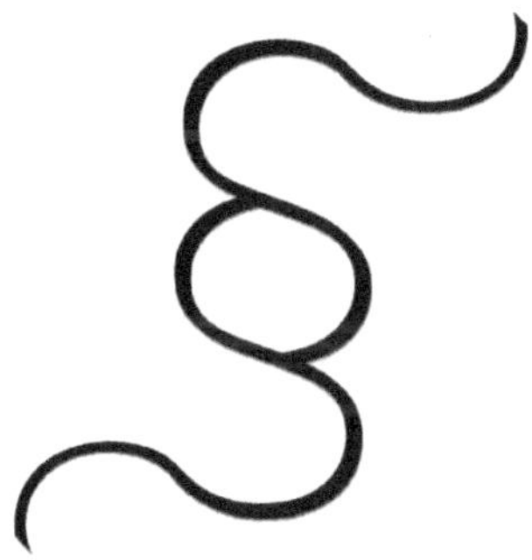

Reneé Bibby's 'Skills in the Domestic Arts'
is available in its entirety at
ThisIsSplice.co.uk/2019/07/22/skills-in-the-domestic-arts

Michael Conley

# An Introduction to
# Michael Conley

Daniel Davis Wood

PENGUINS ARE AMONG the most aggressive animals I've ever known. I have some ignominious experience in this area. In my twenties, unable to find a job doing anything else, I took a position at a zoo where I had the displeasure of dressing up in a six-foot-tall koala costume and parading around the premises for the entertainment of visitors. My route took me past the penguin enclosure more or less every hour. I don't blame the penguins for being alarmed when I approached them in costume, though I remain haunted by the way they huddled together by the glass and flung themselves at it—at me—madly flapping their stubby wings and hissing and clacking their beaks. That said, I've never understood why they showed the same behaviour to me, and me alone, when I passed them again at the end of the day, after I'd taken the costume off and changed back into my civilian clothes. It was as if they could smell the shame on my skin like a sheen of sweat. I figured, then, that if ever any species could or would be inclined to orchestrate a rebellion against humanity, penguinkind would be it. The hatred I saw in Spheniscidae was blind, pure, perfect.

All of which is to say that maybe I was primed to recognise the truth of Michael Conley's 'Krill Rations' when I stumbled upon it online one day. Then again, there's something mesmerising and perversely delightful about the way it's written, this short short story about an uprising of angry penguins, told as it is in diaristic fragments-cum-announcements that track the daily progress of their rebellion. "Day 4," begins a typical entry. "We are aware that the penguins' keening has escalated. Those exposed report un-controllable sobbing as they are reminded of all their unspoken childhood sadnesses. Earplugs and tissues will be issued to all homes within a two-mile radius." How to account for the magic of such a Michael Conley story? If W.H. Auden was early to notice that a gateway to hell could open up from "the crack in the tea-cup," Michael is his descendant. In Michael's story collection, *Flare and Falter*, seemingly innocuous flaws in the fabric of ordinary things lead ultimately to mayhem, entropy, apocalypse. Half the time, the catastrophe unfolds on a world-historical scale and signals the imminent downfall of civilisation; the other half, it's a private life that unravels towards a disastrous conclusion—and it's usually a private life already stunted by the person living it.

I found my way to Michael's stories when, having carried 'Krill Rations' around with me for some months, I saw his name on a list of finalists for the Manchester Writing Competition—a list quite outdated by the time I came across it. The story that landed him a finalist's slot was 'The God Quetzalcoatl Has Retired and Now Runs a Pub in South Manchester.' As advertised, the story finds the "Mesoamerican god of wind and learning" banished from the Aztec city of Tenochtitlan following the fifteenth century Spanish conquest, only to inexplicably wake up in the present day as the publican of the Three Arrows. But here's the other thing about the stories of Michael Conley: for all their apocalypticism—and, in this story, the fall of Tenochtitlan is merely a harbinger for the collapse of Quetzalcoatl's mundane modern life—they are laced with heart, with genuine pathos. I imagine that there are readers who might dismiss Michael Conley, too hastily, as a writer of comic sketches, the literary equivalent of Mitchell and Webb. More's the pity. His work might combine an antic tone with exaggerated imagery and outrageous events, but it blends these elements with a certain sort of tenderness—with real concern for characters who expose their vulnerabilities, no matter how buffoonish they may seem—and it is *this* quality that makes Michael's stories simultaneously farcical and touching. We downplay the value of this alchemy at our peril.

'Big Lads' is red meat Michael Conley. The plus-sized men of the title are living, breathing stereotypes—characterised up-front by the statistically probable likes and dislikes of their demographic, and not even given the dignity of proper names—but their innate humanity breaks through the façade to hilarious effect. All the typical features of a Michael Conley story are here, from the over-the-top similes ("he's large around the chest and walks like a hard-back dictionary") to the ineluctable drift into chaos—as well as the usual lopsidedness of events, the deflationary wheeze of a climax that makes a crescendo of disappointment. And the penguins are at work here, too. No, you can't *see* them. No, they don't appear on the page. But look: they're there, just in another form. They're there in the director's questions, in the stream of queries she hurls at the big lads much as those flightless birds hurl themselves at their captors—needling, provoking, chipping away at superficially solid structures—until the bombardment breaks open a chink in the defences, and suddenly all hell breaks loose.

# Big Lads

The website sells clothes for big lads. The best-selling item on the site is the button-down plaid shirt, which comes in a variety of colours and makes the big lads look and feel like lumberjacks, even though in this economy it's a statistical improbability that any of them are lumberjacks. Other popular items include the brown work boots and the brown fur-collared aviator jacket.

Big lads, according to market research, enjoy rugby, action movies, and barbecues. The statistically probable likes and dislikes of big lads have been reflected in previous online and print advertising. For this, the first televised campaign, some real-life big lads have been chosen to sit together on burgundy Chesterfield sofas and will be filmed engaging in light-hearted small talk about big lad interests, while modelling the newest ranges. It's been decided that four is the optimal number, two big lads per Chesterfield.

All four are white, even though the casting call did emphasise the company's commitment to diversity. All four also have beards. Aside from this, each big lad is big in his own way. Big Lad #1, for example, is easily the biggest: both tall and wide. *Too* big, really, but only slightly, and in a pleasing way, like when you walk into a room and there's a Great Dane in there unexpectedly, and, confused for a second, you mutter to yourself: *what's that little horse doing in here?* Big Lad #2 is not tall, and his arms are actually quite short, but he's large around the chest and walks like a hardback dictionary. His head is shaved and he has three visible folds in the back of his neck. Big Lad #3 looks older than the others: he could play a latter-day Henry VIII; not in a proper film, but maybe in a reconstruction for a low-budget BBC4 history programme, laughing heartily at the head of a table and eating a normal-sized turkey leg that looks, in his hand, like a much smaller turkey leg. Big Lad #4 is the youngest, his shoulder-length brown hair tucked behind his huge ears. He's the only one in shorts, and his almost bare legs are unexpectedly shiny and hairless. He looks as though he could peel a grapefruit with one hand.

The objective is to capture four or five different conversations of around fifteen seconds each, which will then be broadcast on a rotating basis. The conversations will be triggered through prompt questions which include "Which sportsman would you like to be, if you could be a sportsman?", "What superpower do you most wish you could have?" and "What are your top three barbecue seasonings?" The topics of conversation have been selected specifically to ensure the big lads don't seem like weirdos.

There are a couple of false starts. In response to the first question, "Do you like cliffhangers in movies?", Big Lad #1, perched on the arm of the Chesterfield on the left, says, *Well, the cliffhanger has to be a good one. If it's a good one, then yeah, I love them, but if it's just a boring one, no, not for me.* He folds his arms and leans back slightly, looking directly into camera. His smile, which starts off as genuine, freezes after a couple of seconds. The other three big lads nod in agreement, and there is a pause before they all turn to look off-camera at the director.

"Okay, cut," the director says. "That's grand, lads, cheers." She gives them the thumbs up, then carefully tightens her ponytail and maintains a neutral expression. "For the next one, could we try and keep the conversation going a bit?" The big lads nod again. "And just, like, while we're rolling, could you try not to look at me or into the camera? Just look at each other, like you're just at a party or round each other's house or something? That okay?"

Big Lad #3 stands up from the Chesterfield on the right and stretches, yawns, cracks his knuckles. Then he sits back down. *All right*, he says. *Ready.*

The second question is the superpower one. Big Lad #2 leans forward and steeples his fingers under his chin.

*Super strength*, he offers.

*You already look pretty strong*, says Big Lad #1.

Big Lad #2 blushes. *Thanks, man*, he says.

*You know what mine would be?* says Big Lad #4, who hasn't spoken much at all yet, even in the Green Room. The other three look at him expectantly. Thus far, there has been none of the kind of alpha-male jostling that one might have expected from this situation. Nobody has mentioned, for example, Big Lad #4's shiny legs. The big lads are quiet and respectful: in one another, each one seems to see himself, and all other big lads, reflected gloriously. *Mine would be, whenever a piece of food is thrown up in the air, to always be able to catch it in my mouth.* There is another pause, which Big Lad #4 interprets as an invitation to continue. *I mean, I've been practicing it a lot by myself, and I'm already pretty good at it, probably better than the average person. It's harder when someone else throws the food, though, and that's what I'd want the superpower for.*

*Is that a superpower?* asks Big Lad #3.

*Once, when I was about fifteen,* Big Lad #4 continues, leaning forward over the edge of his seat, *I managed it with a fruit polo that my mate threw from the other side of the school hall. I, like, dived for it and caught it straight in my mouth, like I was a seal at Sea World. Everyone went wild. It was probably the purest moment of my life. Even now, lime to me tastes like victory.*

"Okay, cut," the director says. "That's grand, lads, cheers." She takes a couple of deep breaths and picks up a clipboard resting by her elbow. There's only a blank piece of paper attached to it, but she traces her finger down the sheet as if consulting notes. When she speaks again, she keeps her tone light. "We're just going to swap things around a bit, just continuity stuff." At her signal— a subtle nod of the head—an assistant steps forward to whisper into the ear of Big Lad #4, prompting him to rise and then leading him back to the Green Room. As the door swings shut behind him, he takes a last look at the other big lads and waves goodbye, grinning all the while. A different big lad is led out by a different assistant, and he takes Big Lad #4's place on the Chesterfield. He is not quite as tall as Big Lad #1, nor as broad as Big Lad #2, but there is a softness to his hips that suggests substance, and his forehead is extremely wide.

The third question is: "Would you rather be the good cop or the bad cop?" Big Lad #3 fields it first, explaining that although he absolutely respects the necessity for a bad cop in certain contexts, he personally would always prefer to be the good cop, all the way.

*I agree, I've just not got it in me*, says Big Lad #1.

*I think I could do it*, says the new Big Lad #4, *but I wouldn't enjoy it.*

*I'm not being funny*, Big Lad #1 replies, *but we could ALL do it. I mean, look at us. We're all big lads. We could all do it easily.*

The big lads laugh nervously, then look down at their own large frames, study their own forearms, weigh meaty right fists in open left hands. Big Lad #3 pats his pectoral muscle, curling his thick fingers around an imaginary police badge. Each of them can easily imagine how they might expertly angle the lightbulb into the face of the terrorist, while a smaller, wilier partner looks on.

*Good cop*, Big Lad #3 repeats: *All. The. Way.* The nervous smile on his face crumples slightly. The camera zooms into a close up just as his eyes begin to well with tears. His chuckles seem to morph into a series of odd hiccupping yelps. He looks confused, as though his own face is rebelling against him, and it's not long before he's sobbing uncontrollably.

"Okay, cut," the director says. "That's grand, lads, cheers." She moves out from behind the camera and steps awkwardly between the two Chesterfields. To her dismay, she realises that in fact all four of the big lads are crying, shoulders hunched, avoiding any sort of visual or physical contact with each other. She ignores the silent, questioning way some of the assistants seem to be looking at her. "We'll take a break there, shall we?"

The big lads are led back to the Green Room.

DURING LUNCH, there's a short discussion between the director and her assistants about whether it might be best to employ a completely new set of big lads. They have used the only substitute they had on the premises, so an assistant is sent out to retrieve the audition headshots from the recycling bin. It doesn't work: immediately they all remember why these rejects were rejected in the first place. Nose too delicate. Tiny squirrel ears. Beautiful emerald green eyes. Patchy beard.

It's decided, then, reluctantly, that there is some footage from the morning that can still be salvaged and used, given judicious cutting, and that it would be better to try and push on with the resources at hand. It's agreed that there will be no more questions about cops, or about being good or bad. The big lads are brought back out to the Chesterfields.

"What's your best party trick?" an assistant shouts, doing his best to sound enthusiastic. The big lads grin at each other and nod eagerly.

"Action!" shouts the director.

Big Lad #1 stands up.

*Watch this,* he says. He begins a slow handclap, and the other three oblige him by continuing it. He unbuttons his red and black plaid lumberjack shirt. The camera zooms in upon his small, surprisingly hairless belly, and he rolls it so that a horizontal crease in the fat dances up and down his torso. As the camera zooms out, though, it's immediately clear that Big Lad #1 is crying again, even as he continues rolling his belly quicker and quicker to the beat of the clapping.

*Woo hoo!* shouts Big Lad #2, but the whoop turns quickly into a howl of anguish and he falls to his knees, still clapping in time.

*That's hilarious!* says Big Lad #3, his baritone voice thick with tears.

The new Big Lad #4 remains seated, focusing on his own index finger, which he has bent right back so that his fingernail touches his forearm. *Double-jointed*, he bawls over the clapping and sobbing, but the others don't seem to hear him.

"Okay, cut," the director says. "That's grand, lads, cheers." She picks up her water bottle and squeezes it tightly. "Can I just ask..." she trails off and waits patiently for the big lads to compose themselves and sit back down on the Chesterfields. Some assistants offer tissues. The bottle is three quarters full, but she drains it all in large gulps before the big lads appear to have fully recovered. She crushes it in her fist and turns to them with an expansive, open-armed gesture. "Can I just ask, lads, what's the problem here?"

The big lads look at each other and shrug.

*What problem?* the new Big Lad #4 asks. *Was that not okay?*

"No, no, lads, it was great," the director replies. "We can definitely use all the footage right up to the crying. But, also, could we maybe try doing it, you know, without..."

*Without what?* says Big Lad #3.

"Without the crying?"

*Sure*, say the other three big lads, speaking almost in unison and nodding in actual unison.

The director snatches a clipboard from the nearest assistant and scans the list of questions herself. She immediately skips "What were you most terrified of as a child?", which seems to be asking for trouble. Same with "Describe a time when you may have inadvertently harmed somebody you loved," which really should've been crossed out during the lunch break. Conversely, "What are your views on double denim?" seems too banal, even for a fifteen-second advert for menswear. "Do you want children?" and "What do you love most about your body?" both seem too intrusive, too provocative. In the periphery of her vision, she can see the big lads begin to fidget a little, and she notices a tension creeping into their postures.

She sighs.

She asks, "What's the best type of puppy?"

The camera starts rolling again.

Big Lad #3 smiles and says, *I love puppies. Definitely a dog person.*

The other big lads murmur assent: they, too, are dog people.

*Probably Labradors for me*, says the new Big Lad #4. *Big daft golden retriever.*

*What are the ones that look like wolves?* Big Lad #2 asks. The other big lads stir excitedly in their seats.

*Ooh yeah, huskies*, says Big Lad #1. *Love huskies.*

Big Lad #3 nods dreamily. *Amazing blue eyes*, he says.

Big Lad #1 leans back on the Chesterfield, looking into the middle distance.

There's a short pause. All the big lads have the same expression on their faces: their lips are pursed tightly and sweat is beading on their brows. They all begin to redden, not with embarrassment, but with effort. All of them are holding their breath, looking back and forth between one another, eyes widening as each big lad recognises his own torment in the desperate, imploring faces of his fellows. The kinship they seemed to feel at the beginning of the day is still there, but now it has twisted into something grotesque. They see each other too clearly, too intimately, as though staring into a fresh wound. They see each other as themselves metastasised, as if they've been smashed together into one single screaming solid mountain of big lad flesh and bone. They see each other's untold histories and probable futures, secret shames and lifelong irritations.

*Sixteen pounds, three ounces*, a doctor whispers to an exhausted new mother.

*Fucking hell!* countless smaller men exclaim. *What've they been feeding you then, eh?*

At school, bespoke PE kits.

In the pub, the automatic assumption of an interest in real ales.

Then, inescapably, the jars. So, so many jars, packed with so many juicy treats, with so many lids crying out to be twisted loose.

Big Lad #3 exhales first in a great wet rush of emotion. *B-b-beagles!* he shouts, too loudly, before gulping down another breath of air and forcing his lips back together. He's trembling. *B-beagles!* he shouts again, a real outburst this time, *and b-b-basset hounds with the droopy ears!*

None of them can contain it any longer. The tears begin to flow freely even as they continue to swallow their sobs. They do not wipe their faces. Big Lad #2 is still holding his breath; his eyes are popping out and his lips are turning blue. Big Lad #3 looks to the ceiling with an upturned gaze as if praying for guidance from the god of big lads. Big Lads #1 and #4 have both slid down their respective Chesterfields onto the floor and have assumed the foetal position.

The room is silent. The silence isn't quite *silent* silence, not you-could-hear-a-pin-drop silence, but the tense kind of silence you get in a room full of big lads crying so hard, in such despair, that they can't actually make a sound anymore.

"Okay, cut," the director says. "That's grand, lads." She sighs, and shakes her head, and mumbles: "Cheers."

*from*

# The Village Where Everyone Keeps Punching Themselves in the Mouth

THE GUYS IN THE OFFICE LAUGHED when you were assigned this one. You'll know them by their scabbed knuckles, they said, by their clawed right hands cradled always at chest level like twitching beach-rescued starfish.

And they won't tell you anything.

You start with their Wikipedia page. There's surprisingly little on the whole 'punching themselves in the mouth' issue. You have to scroll right down to the heading at the bottom: 'Controversy':

> In late 2016, the media reported extensively on an "epidemic of self-harm"[1] supposedly "sweeping" the village. Although the stories were on this occasion sensationalist in tone and largely exaggerated, many were correct to note that there is a long-established and widely-misunderstood tradition of the cultural practice of mouth-punching that has always been observed by residents of this area of the country.[citation needed]

No further explanation and nothing at all on the rapid spread of the practice over the last eighteen months.

The rest of the page is less than useless, written with the pedantry of the kind of amateur local historian who will no doubt head straight for you in the pub on your first night. There are several paragraphs on the village's medieval origins, a section on the successful protest against the construction of a sand quarry in the late nineties, and a list of every single bus, with numbers, that travels to the slightly larger towns dotted throughout the region. There's even a section entitled 'Notable People', although it consists of only a single name, an archery bronze medallist from the Rio Olympics in 2016.

"They're so weird about that archery guy, as well." You jump at the sound of the voice so close to your ear. Arkley is standing behind you, reading over your shoulder. You hate it when she does that. Arkley scouted out the village a year and a half ago, when the first reports trickled in. You should probably schedule some sort of debrief with her, if you want to play this by the book.

You minimise the Wikipedia tab and turn to face her. "What do you mean?"

She takes a bite from her foil-wrapped breakfast burrito. A drupelet of scrambled egg plops onto your keyboard. "Everyone under thirty claims they were in his class at school," she says. "He lives in London and has never been back. And listen to this: after he picked up his bronze medal, the village painted all the post-boxes gold even though Royal Mail specifically asked them not to."

You don't reply. She pats you on the shoulder, almost sympathetically. "You'll love it there. Have a good time." She swaggers away, chuckling.

You spend the rest of the morning in the archives, looking over Arkley's reports, which is almost as bad as spending time with her. You wince at every spelling mistake, every homophone error. They are so frequent that you suspect she probably went back into the files last night and planted them all there just to irritate you.

YOU'VE BEEN IN THE JOB way too long to be idealistic any more. You're not going to get to the bottom of this. You're going to stay in a B&B just outside the village for the maximum three nights it will take you to write your report, and then you're going to leave.

Still, that first night in the pub does shock you with its unpleasantness, despite your natural detachment and the details in Arkley's reports that were supposed to make you feel prepared. You walk in and endure the obligatory stranger-entering-a-saloon moment. All conversations fall into silence and every face turns towards you. But then the impact of this moment is ruined by the fact that it coincides with an 'everyone-punching-themselves-in-the-mouth' moment. They've been doing this so long now that their cycles appear to be fully synchronised and they all do it at the same time so that the wet thudding squelch is amplified, like the noise of a muddy football kicked hard into a naked belly.

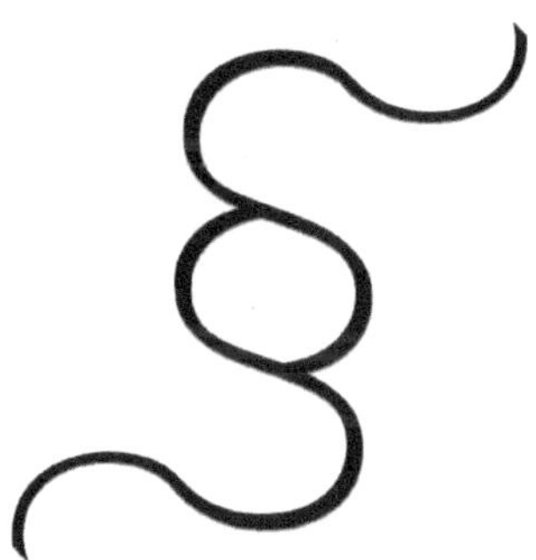

Michael Conley's 'The Village Where Everyone
Keeps Punching Themselves in the Mouth'
is available in its entirety at
ThisIsSplice.co.uk/2018/07/30/the-village

Abi Hynes

# An Introduction to
# Abi Hynes

Michael Conley

I'VE KNOWN ABI HYNES for a few years, from various literary nights around Manchester. Manchester has a brilliant live literature scene and Abi is a big part of it: she used to run First Draft, which I read at, and she has read at my night, The Other. She's one of those writers you're always excited to see turning up to an open mic because you know she's going to bring quality every time.

One of my favourite stories of hers is a flash fiction piece called 'The Gastrosophist,' which you can find online at Boudicca Press. There's no point in me spoiling it by revealing too much, but suffice to say it's about an *unusual* meal, and it's really not for the faint-hearted. In fact, you should probably stick to bread and water for twenty-four hours before and after reading it, just to be on the safe side. I love that it's not only gross and disturbing (and it is) but also deeply moral as well, which I feel is important if you're going to explore the grotesque places this story takes its readers. But the prose is lavish, sensual, and perfectly paced, too:

proof that the best flash writers need only a thousand words to do what others struggle to achieve in a hundred thousand.

Abi's work is difficult to pin down, genre-wise, and that's what I love about it: it plays fast and loose with genre expectations, which means that each of her stories has a great capacity for surprise. There are elements of horror here and there, and sci-fi/fantasy as well, but Abi also has a keen eye for realistic details and natural dialogue. Her writing is of a sort that isn't afraid to break rules. Another story, 'The Pure of Heart,' is a good example of this. It begins with a wryly funny, realistic depiction of a teenage girl in a nightclub in Preston, where she has a depressing encounter with an inadequate man named Mike (which I'm choosing not to interpret as a slur on all Mikes), but within a few hundred words the girl has stepped through a portal into a fantasy world and drifted into the territory of Le Guin or Jemisin. But then the story turns again, packing a strange emotional punch, and *then*, because it's so short, the ending just leaves you there, helpless, slightly confused—but it's all done so skilfully that you've almost forgotten you weren't reading a sci-fi/fantasy epic all along. What's truly brilliant is that at no point does the story attempt to explain or justify itself, which I think a story by a less confident writer would have tried and inevitably failed to do.

Which brings me to the story in this anthology. I was delighted when I first read this; there's so much in it. It reminds me a bit of Ted Chiang's 'Story of Your Life,' only darker and nastier, more sinister. Presented entirely through dialogue, it asks the reader to piece together the backstory that has brought its two speakers to a meeting point, but the real pleasure is in the way the language shifts and twists, especially as the speakers try to find common ground from two alien positions. The bureaucratic tone of the speaker on the left morphs into something else, more panicked, as the "conversation" progresses. The "alienness" of the speaker on the right becomes more pronounced as he/she/it gives more consideration to the other speaker's human concerns. This is a story that does all the things I love about sci-fi—it world-builds, it plays with words; it's disturbing and funny—while also clearly addressing our political moment with its themes of colonial arrogance, border disputes, and a fundamental miscommunication between two seemingly irreconcilable worldviews. And with that in mind: do we cheer at the end? I think we might do.

# A conversation recorded before the end of the experiment

FIRST, we feel we ought to recognise
that the adjustment period has been
difficult for both sides. We knew there
would be challenges and we prepared
for those as best we could, but there
have also been difficulties we did not
foresee. And we acknowledge that
there were no plans in place where in
hindsight we ought to have anticipated
certain... eventualities. And this has
caused suffering for all concerned.

Hind. Sight.

Yes. A wonderful thing, as they say.

What is—?

Oh, of course. My apologies. Hindsight.
To, um—to look back, behind you, at the
path that has brought you to this point.

If we'd known then what we know now.
We would have done things differently.

> To look behind you.

Yes.

> To look back.
> At your hind legs?

Well.
I suppose so.
In a manner of speaking.

> Okay.

Okay?

> Nodding. We are nodding.
> That we hear and understand
> what you are saying though not
> necessarily that we agree.
> Yes?

Yes?

> That is the correct way
> to mean the nodding?

It's—yes, it's a start. That we are
listening and understanding each
other—that's an important start.
I think we can agree on that!

> We are nodding.

Okay, then.
So.
One of the things I think I should
explain is that it was a shock to most
of us when we arrived and saw you
for the first time. In the flesh, as it
were. You see, there was propaganda
back home. We'd been told you were
not so different from us.
And of course that's true in some
ways, we do have plenty in common.
But you see, at first sight...
They'd used the word—it's offensive,
I know, I see that now—but the
messaging back home used the word
*humanoid*, and that led us to think...

You thought we
would be having legs.

It... It surprised us that you didn't.
That you don't.
Among... other things.
It was just a bit of a shock, really, and
I think that—that shock—it frightened
some of us, and that's why some of us
didn't behave as we, *they*, ought to
have done. But then of course—and I'm
not making excuses for those initial
settlers here—we must remember that
this is the very first time two parties
have tried to share a clean world. There
were bound to be teething problems.

That we do not agree.
Our teeth are not
a problem.

Well. Not for you, perhaps. But for us—

Our teeth are not
a problem.

It's...
It's an expression. It's an idiom, which...
which... complicates things, I realise.
I'm sorry.
I mean simply to say that there were
bound to be some problems.
To begin with.

Bound to be.

Inevitably.

To be.
Bound?

Well...
Look.
Perhaps—perhaps we—
perhaps that's where we should begin.

To be bound.

Boundaries. The bounds. Our
territories, and the marking of borders.

                                        It will not help,
                                        this marking.

We think it might.
If boundaries are to be enforced—

                                        How is it you would
                                        enforce boundaries
                                        against us?

Enforce?

                                        You said:
                                        En.
                                        Force.

Oh. I see.
I see the misunderstanding.
Look.
We're not talking about anything
involving actual physical force.
Quite the opposite, in fact.
Boundaries can be maintained
simply by mutual agreement.

                                        Enforced without.

Without what?

                                        Force.

Quite.
Well, yes.
Exactly.

The point is. What we want—what we
all want, surely—is to keep our two
*peoples* peacefully apart. We think that
should be perfectly possible. All we
need is your co-operation.

Co-operation.<br>
Meaning?<br>
Collective. Operation.<br>
Yes?

Exactly that.

This we cannot do.

I...

Might I ask why not?

One world we are sharing.<br>
Only one. What will you do<br>
with your borders?<br>
Cut this world and make two?<br>
It is not possible.<br>
We read that where you come<br>
from there are piece-lands.

Peace-lands?

Small pieces of land,<br>
separated by sea.

Oh! Islands.

Yes, yes. Eye-lands.

Because you see them
but you cannot reach them
without a plan—yes?
These eye-lands.
We do not have these.
What you sow over there will
change the grazing of the
livestock we keep here.
It is like a man. It is like you.
If I tear you, you will die.

That's true, but—but we're not
suggesting any—anything like
that. It's just a question of
differentiating where we can go
and where you can go. There is a
method, I'm told, of harmlessly
changing the colour of soil so
that everyone knows: if I'm on
red soil, that's fine; I am safe and
I'm allowed to be here. But if I
look down and I see that the soil
is blue...

What is this colour?

I'm sorry?
I thought you could... They
told us you could see in colour.

We can see so.
We understand a woman when
she says: *most plants are green.*

We have seen this green,<br>
but it is not one thing.<br>
One plant has many parts.<br>
They are all themselves.<br>
Yet this woman says:<br>
*all of this is green.*<br>
So we ask her:<br>
what is green?

I see.

And so, to you, we ask:<br>
what is blue?<br>
The soil is made of millions of<br>
fragments, and they are all<br>
themselves.<br>
How can they all be blue?

I see.
Yes, I see.
You know, this is exactly why
we need a dialogue.
We've just learnt something
there, about you, that we never
would've thought of on our own.
The soil idea—that's no good then.
So what? We'll throw it out. We'll
throw out as many ideas as we
need to, and when we find the right
one, it will be based on mutual
understanding and respect.

*Ressspect.*<br>
We have not heard this before.

Well, it means...
To believe that another party is
important. That they are—at
least—equal to oneself.
To treat them with dignity.

> Your blue soil.
> This would give you dignity?

As I say,
it doesn't have to be the soil.

> But your soils would show
> that you and we are equal.

Yes. That's really central, actually.
That's what it all comes down to at
the end of the day. To be friends,
we must be equals.

> We see.
> But why only when it is dark?

I'm sorry?

> You would like us to be equal
> only at the end of the day?

No, no. I don't mean...
It's an idiom.

> Do you mean only for this day,
> or is it for all days that you are
> speaking?

It's just an expression.

> Yes. We are laughing.

Oh?
I can't hear—

> Inside.
> Inside ourselves, we are doing
> what we think you call laughing.

Oh.
Why?

> We are amused.
> We are teasing you with these
> questions about the end of the day.

Ah, okay. That's fine.
A bit of levity. That's fine.

> But also we laugh because we
> cannot think you equal to us.

Excuse me?
What do you mean by that, exactly?

> You may think that we are
> equal friends. You may give us
> your dignite—your dignutt—

Dignity.

> Dignity.
> But we cannot.

Well, then.
I think we've arrived at
another of these examples.
It's our language barrier
interfering again. Or it's our
cultural differences showing!
You see, if I didn't know
better, I could take offence at
what you just said.
It sounded like you were
saying you think we're
beneath you. Our species.

> Yes.
> These are the sounds
> we mean to make.

Oh. I see.
Perhaps...
Perhaps this is a subject we can
come back to, after we've given
more thought to the practicalities.
I have a list here. Points to discuss.
Agenda items. Let me see...
Food supplies?
We're all concerned about food,
aren't we?

> We are not so concerned.

But it's an issue, isn't it?
It's a problem.

Neither of us seems to have
anticipated quite how quickly
certain shortages would emerge.
And we did think we had agreed—
I mean, it's in the initial settlement
contract, isn't it?
The terms for dividing and
managing the food supply.
If you'd care to have another
look at the document—

>                    This is not necessary.

No, please. Be my guest. I insist.
Jenny?
Jenny here—Jenny? Don't be
silly, it's fine. Jenny is going to
pass it through the secure
window for you.
That's it.

>                    We have read this previously.

If you'd care to look—clause
four, right there. You'll see it
was agreed that both sides
would commit to a plant-based
diet until livestock imports
had reached a level sufficient
to allow the establishment of
sustainable populations.

>                    We have read this.

Can you explain to me, then,
why your side felt you couldn't
abide by that agreement?

It is not good,
this translation here.

It was discussed at great length,
before it was agreed. Wasn't it?
I mean—
What are you saying, exactly?
That part of the settlement
contract wasn't properly
understood by your leadership?

It is understood.
But it is very badly phrased.
Who did this?

I don't think I have a name to
give you just now. It was all done
very officially, though.
I can assure you of that.
Are you saying you would like
a new translation?

No.

So, then?

Yes?

Can you explain to me why you,
your *people*, felt it impossible to
abide by the agreement?

For instance—and I realise it
might be controversial to bring
this up but I really think it's the
elephant in the—
Never mind. Ignore that.
My question to you is: what
happened to the people onboard
the 917?

>                                        This was unfortunate.

Yes. It was.
There are all sorts of rumours
that we have not exactly
managed to contain. I would
never have believed them but
I saw the drone footage, and...
Well, I was frightened. A lot
of people found it very
frightening because it just
doesn't seem to make any
sense. Can you explain it to me?

>                                        We were very hungry.

You must see—
Jenny, no. It's all right.
It's all right.
Look.
You must see why we don't feel
that that, your *hunger*, justifies
your actions.

We do not know what you feel.
We have our own feelings.


Well, look. Tell me this, at least.
Why did our new arrivals behave
the way they did when they
came into contact with you?
Was something said?
Were threats made?
Were they poisoned or was
there—did you release some
sort of inhalant to make them
suggestible, or immune to pain?
To rob them of their wits?


We did not do any of these things.


Then what?
This is very—
Wait.
What is that? I'm hearing—
Is that—
What I'm hearing now,
is *that* laughter?


Our laughter is no longer inside us.


You're laughing at me?


At your people.


My people?


We remember them.

The ones you took.

                                        We remember them.

Do you?
I remember. Watching
them arrive. After waiting
for their arrival for so long.
Seeing that crowd of you
there, encircling them.
Do you know how
traumatic that was?
They knew what had been
happening—they knew
what it meant, as soon as
they saw you. But they
walked towards you as
calm, as placid, as docile as—

                                                Yes?

I can't say it.

                            Your language is deficient, then.

There was a man I used to
work with. I saw him
dismembered and devoured.
His arm was ripped off and
fed to one of your offspring.
He didn't even flinch. He just
waited for you to come back
for the rest of him.

I saw a woman unbutton her
uniform to expose her torso.
Then she just stood there as
she was sliced open, navel to
sternum, and had her organs
extracted.

They were consumed.

But how did you do it?

It is not possible to say.

So, then, how do we broker
peace? How do we find a
way forward if we can't be
sure that it won't happen
again? If we don't even
know what weapon it is you
have at your disposal that
can do something like that,
let alone get you to
surrender it? How do we—
how do we do it if we can't
get an assurance that this
atrocity was just, you know,
just a skirmish, a mis-
understanding? Part of the
teething problems.
Do you understand my
dilemma? *Our* dilemma?

We understand it.

And are you *nodding*?

We do not know.  
If we can help you.  
In the way you want.

We need an answer. You  
see that, don't you? Today,  
between us—we have the  
power to deliver  
reassurances.  
For instance—  
What about our  
settlement? Can we talk  
about New Copenhagen?

This *new* confuses us.  
We have never seen this first  
Copenhagen.  
This one is for us the first  
Copenhagen.

Are you teasing me again?  
Do you call it something else?

We do not call it.  
It is not a dog, which you teach  
a sound to make it come to you,  
as I have seen in your archives.  
We are not like you.  
We do not name a thing  
because we have seen it.

Yes, yes. All right.
Shall we stick to our name
for the place, then, if your
people haven't given it one?
We might struggle to
make progress if we can't
even refer to places.

If we did refer to it,
you would not be able
to pronounce.

Well, *all right* then.
New Copenhagen—as we
call it. We'd like to clarify
whether your actions
there have been in order
to claim that particular
territory?
To take it from us?
We thought—I thought—
Some of us thought you
meant for your hostility to
be taken as a show of
strength, that's all.
A play for dominance.

We are nodding.

Nodding at what?

At your words.

Which words? Which bit?

> The words that say we meant
> to show you our dominance.

I'm right?
You're confirming this?

> We do not need to show
> what is a fact.

And—
Oh, God.
And this is the official
line? If this is the official
line, then—
New Copenhagen, what
happened there last week.
Is an act of warfare.

> Warfare.

*Warfare.*

> War.
> Fare.
> As in: to pay?
> A toll?

I really don't have a clue
about the etymology of
that word. And frankly,
I think it's distracting us
from what's really
important here.

The lives of each of our
peoples are depending on the
outcome of this conversation.
They're the important things
for us to focus on.

Important?
This is not the word we use.

Perhaps—

*Interesting.*
This is the word we use.
Your lives are *interesting* to us.
Not important.

And this is—again—
this is the official line?
You're speaking on behalf of
the leadership?
Can you tell me...
I hope I'm not being
impertinent when I ask this,
but—what's your role?
I mean, where are you in
the hierarchy?
What level of expertise do
you have, to negotiate our
future cohabitation?

It is difficult. To translate.

Try me.

I am one who—
how is it said by you?—
*accumulates.*

Accumulates what?

Knowledge.

Knowledge of?

Life.
The life of the world.

I don't understand.

Life. *Forms.*
You say: *I study*. Life forms.
Other than ourselves.

You mean—
You're a student?

I wish to accumulate
knowledge of your people.

You're just a student.

While the opportunity
remains open.
While you remain here
in sufficient numbers.

Oh, God.

Oh. God?

What have we done?

                              Are we intended
to answer this question?

What have we done?
What have we—?

                          Your words are continuing but
they are not moving forward.

What have we done?
Oh, God, what have—
what can we—what are we
supposed to—
Oh, God. A fucking *student?*

                        This *fucking*—this you are using
for emphasis? I did not know.
Your species: I find it very
*fucking* interesting.

Help me. Oh, God.
Help us all.

                              Do you wish for us to
end our talking now?

Can you—
Okay.
Just give me a minute.
You have to understand.
I had hoped...
No, that doesn't matter.

They sent you. A student.
This wasn't easy to arrange.
And they sent *you*.
But can you—
You can at least take a
message back, can't you?
You can go back to the
leadership and tell them,
from me, tell them...

If you wish it.

I do. I do wish it. Very much.
Tell them...
Look, I'm sorry. I'm sorry
I got upset just now.
These are difficult times.
I just—I'm sure...
I'm sure they are difficult
on your side too.
I want you to tell them
we'd still like to work
towards partnership.
Collaboration.

Co-operation.

Yes. Yes, that's right.
We don't want a war.

No. You do not.

We only want to set some
boundaries, you see?

You mustn't think of them
as anything but the
foundations of a
friendship.
Take this window
between us now,
for instance. It doesn't
only separate us. It allows
us to sit face-to-face.
It has made this
conversation possible.

              This is the message we should convey?

Yes. Yes, but listen.
Understand it first.
All right?
Look at this glass.
Look at what it does.
Look at what it *allows* us
to do in one another's
company. You are there
and I am here and we can
talk like equals because
we both know we are safe.
And it will take time, of
course, to build walls this
strong, if that's what's
needed, across our
territories, however we
agree to map them out.
But when we come to a clean
world, we are rich in time.

We can start small,
and we can slowly expand
our boundaries until our
respective peoples have
their own protected spaces
in which to live. And even
if it is the work of many
generations, well, what
does it matter? Just think
what we might accomplish
next, after all those lifetimes
of working together!

                                        We understand your message.


Tell them—tell them that
our ability to apply ourselves
to a common goal will bring
my people and your people as
close as any neighbours could
hope to be. It will be just like
this, all the world over.

                                              Very good.


A whole world that works
just like this room.
Borders between our
territories, fixed but
crystal clear, functioning
exactly like this pane of
glass, through which we
can talk, and trade,
and share ideas.

This glass:
you must take it down now.

What?
Oh, yes.
I must.

The button is there, by your wrist.

Yes.
I see.
Thank you.

*from*

# Rosie

I WASN'T SUPPOSED TO BE left unsupervised with Rosie. But her handlers had clocked off for the evening and the rest of the crew were tucked up in their trailers, so I seized my chance for some alone time.

At first, I only watched her. She'd been my body double and my muse for nearly eight months, but still I found her inexhaustibly fascinating. I sat opposite her—I was her weaker, paler mirror image—and watched as she toyed with a piece of melon rind, her fingernails picking at tiny pieces of its remaining flesh and bringing them to her lips.

Monkey school, we called it; all our doubles were really apes. We treated them like celebrities. We spent our time off-camera photographing them and begging to be allowed to hug them, just this once. But none of them were quite as clever as my Rosie, who knew me and rushed to meet me in the mornings, who always got the best takes, who was first back into her crate when it was time to close up for the day. I was smitten. I could be forgiven, surely, for this illegal visit, given just how much I loved her.

Every few seconds, Rosie's black eyes flicked up as she checked on me. After fifteen minutes, she huffed out a breath of acknowledgement and shuffled closer.

I mimicked her. It was habit now; she moved, I moved. We rolled our shoulders up and back. Our knuckles kneaded the concrete floor to pitch our weight forwards. I'd wondered if she'd recognise me without my prosthetics, but the connection between us made my scalp fizz. Her expression was like a book written in a foreign language; I knew there was great meaning there if only I could read it.

Earlier that day, we'd had to stop shooting for an hour because something had upset the apes. We'd watched Rosie with another chimp, a more nervous creature than my counterpart, as they shot a scene in which they had to jump down, threatening and ready for battle, from the roof of a stationary train carriage. The other actors and I were waiting to take our turn, sweating inside our furry costumes. We were just changing places when one of the camera guys leapt out at me wearing a gorilla mask, howling in my face and pounding his fists against his chest. I jumped and made him bellow with laughter, then he slapped me on the back and wandered off to find someone else to shock.

It had only been a joke, but Rosie didn't know that. A split second after her handler had clanked shut the door of her travel cage, Rosie screamed and threw her whole weight in the direction of the masked cameraman. Her handler yelled and toppled backwards. Rosie was inconsolable with rage; she wrenched at the bars, yanking backwards and forwards so she almost tipped the crate on its side, and her screeching set off all the other apes. From what seemed like every corner of the set they screamed and hammered and bashed themselves against the bars and walls of their little prisons like they'd all gone instantly mad, and their handlers stared at each other in shock before they set off between the animals with their electric prods, jabbing mercilessly until the rebellion subsided.

*What happened?* they asked. *What set them off?* Nobody seemed to know. I kept my mouth shut, but as they wheeled Rosie away I watched her slumped, dark body get smaller and smaller with a potent mixture of love and shame. She had been trying to defend me; I was certain of it. I had to see with my own eyes that she was all right. Or, if I was being really honest with myself, I felt more than just concern. I felt guilt. I felt that she had been hurt because of me, and somehow I had to make it right between us.

Crouched on the floor of the trailer, I let Rosie's solemn gaze engulf me. We were almost nose to nose. She pressed her beautiful, so-nearly-human face against the bars so that her soft lips bulged between them. I pushed my own forwards, imagining her strength in my jaw. Beneath, her breasts hung smooth and slack, long dark nipples dipping into the fur of her belly. We breathed together: in, and out. I could see my own rapture reflected in her pupils.

Abi Hynes' 'Rosie'
is available in its entirety at
ThisIsSplice.co.uk/2019/07/24/rosie

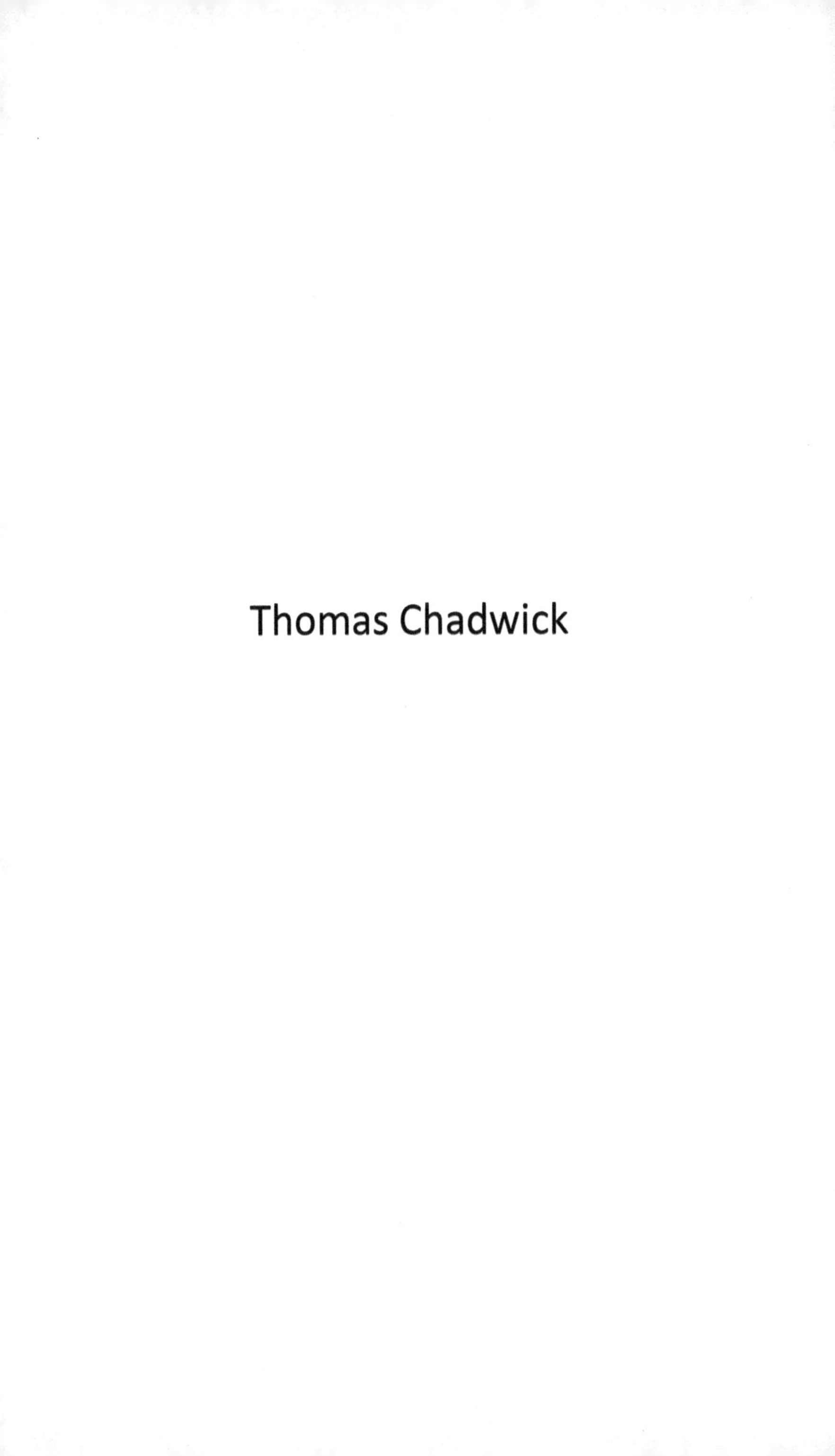

Thomas Chadwick

# An Introduction to
# Thomas Chadwick

Daniel Davis Wood

LIKE MANY OTHER INSOMNIACS, I dread the very stillness I crave. In the hours approaching the time for sleep, I pray—inasmuch as an atheist can pray—that when my head comes to rest on the pillow at last, I will be blessed with tranquillity and won't fall victim to racing thoughts. But then as the hours roll on, as midnight approaches and gives way to early morning, as I wander across the threshold from end-of-day fatigue to untimely wakefulness, I find that everything around me is as tranquil as anyone could hope for: I'm in a space of alert non-happening, a space of encompassing stillness in which my insistent inner voice raises its pitch. And because I know I can't stand it, night after night I lay down in fear of it. When I take to rest, even as I hunger for the stasis I know I'll enter in the pre-dawn dark, I try, in advance, to plot my escape.

On the back cover of Thomas Chadwick's story collection *Above the Fat*, the blurb describes Thomas' characters as the denizens of a "twilit realm": hapless folk whose habitual state of mind is much like mine at the witching hour. It's true. I discovered Thomas' work when his story 'Birch' won a place on the shortlist for the *White Review* Prize in 2017, and his protagonist, Stuart, won a place in my heart. Stuart is heir to a lumber business during the early years of Tony Blair's New Labour government, and he buys into the *faux*-aspirational rhetoric of the times. This means that he looks back on his life with resentment at the path not taken, a path that would have no doubt brought him greater prosperity—he could've been "a damn fine lawyer"—and so, at the same time, he looks forward, too far forward, casting about for a sure investment to make up for lost opportunities, and settles on a scheme to plant birch trees that won't yield profits for at least a decade. He's stuck between two temporal spaces, leading a purgatorial existence, left to himself to wait out the grindingly slow passage of time. But this causes him more pain than he can tolerate. He, too, plots an escape of sorts, acting on an infatuation with a woman in Sweden who offers him hope of a new life. His scheme is laughably irrational, unreason-able, but so what? Trust me: it's also *exactly* the sort of thing that seems reasonable in the endless white night of an insomniac's life. And, rather than rescuing him from his folly, Thomas decides to leave him right there, in limbo, bringing 'Birch' to an end with poor Stuart still suspended, as if encased, in a bubble of time.

As it goes for Stuart, so it goes for many of the other characters in *Above the Fat.* There are Simon and Julius in 'And the Glass Cold Against His Face,' both of them clinging to the ledge of a high-rise tower as the minutes tick by: they think back on the events that have brought them to this point, they think of the grisly future awaiting them on the pavement below, but Thomas leaves them right there, exposed to the elements, their fates unresolved. There are Sam and James in 'A Sense of Agency,' walking alongside the Thames while the floodwaters rise, left behind by Thomas as the waves reach their feet, and there's Jack in the diner in 'Death Valley Junction,' doomed to watch the other patrons receive their lunch orders while he remains hungry, but expecting to be served soon, seemingly for all eternity. There's Stan, 'in 'Stan, Standing,' stuck in front of the mirror, toying with his cufflinks, paralysed by the endless pingings of a neural network overrun with memories and anticipations; there's the chef in 'Above the Fat,' lingering over a frying pan while returning his thoughts to his father's disappearing years; and then, of course, there's Paul, immobilised in Greece for an indeterminate time, in the protracted liminality of 'Red Sky at Night.' *Above the Fat* surveys a congregation of lost souls who have slipped into waking dreams that consciousness can't dissipate.

Now there's Liv in 'The Unsuccessful Candidate,' and maybe also the title character—or, then again, maybe not. Whose tormenting stasis colours this story? That of the anti-Bartleby, the man who fails to land a job but turns up at work anyway, only to spend his days pretending to do tasks he hasn't been assigned? Or that of the woman whose life erodes before her very eyes, whose house disappears, whose bicycle flees, whose place in her own existence might be even more provisional than the place of her not-quite-colleague in the team she thought she belonged to? And, as always with Thomas Chadwick, even language itself can't struggle free of the vortex that drags his people into limbo. How many questions in 'The Unsuccessful Candidate' fall flat, rather than inflecting, to become mere statements without affect? How many exchanges of dialogue involve characters speaking to one another but not truly communicating, letting words sail past their intended recipients like two trains on parallel tracks heading in opposite directions? Small talk about stag nights stirs up fury that nobody validates; idle inquiries into career trajectories are met with mumbles about Robert Mugabe. And don't bother hoping that the bright new dawn of some epiphany will revitalise the half-humans who populate this little corner of Thomas' twilit realm. For all the comic verve—sometimes slapstick, often deadpan—the dawn is still a long way off, always just beyond the horizon of the hours yet to come.

# The Unsuccessful Candidate

A WEEK AFTER THE INTERVIEWS the unsuccessful candidate showed up at the office. He walked across the room and sat down at the spare desk opposite Liv. At first Liv hardly noticed, but when she returned from the kitchen he was still sat there with his back to the desk, staring out across the room as everyone arrived for work.

The unsuccessful candidate was dressed in the same grey suit he'd worn to his interview a week earlier. He wore the same white shirt and polished brown shoes and his tie was the same pale blue that looked as if it had been dusted with sugar. Liv remembered noticing that tie as he'd waited outside Jane's office to be called in. She remembered thinking that, while it was a very nice tie, it was probably too flashy for someone working in accounts and it was no surprise to her when Jane and Mr. Daniels chose to employ someone else.

Liam Langton had started the previous Thursday. He jogged across the office carrying an energy drink and hurled his gym kit under his desk. Liam was a member of a successful five-a-side team and had already told Liv a number of things about West Ham United that she had no wish to know. When Liam bustled in that morning, he found the unsuccessful candidate at the adjacent desk. The unsuccessful candidate held a pen and was rolling it back and forth between his fingers as he stared out across the office. Liam simply nodded at him and logged on to his computer.

The unsuccessful candidate was still there after lunch. When Liv got back from the supermarket where she and Fran went to buy the sandwiches they always intended to make at home, she found him sprawled across the desk with his head on his arms. There was an empty sandwich packet in the bin by his desk and he must have made himself a coffee while they were out because one of the mugs from the kitchen sat beside the monitor.

"Who is he?" Liam asked in the kitchen as he took another energy drink from the fridge.

"They're restructuring in the Birmingham office," Fran said. "Probably something to do with that."

Liam shrugged and started gulping his energy drink. His Adam's apple bobbed like a body beneath a duvet. Liv took her coffee back to her desk and studied the man at the spare desk. He wasn't from Birmingham. He was definitely the unsuccessful candidate from the week before. He sat there with his head still at rest on his folded arms. Only at five did he get to his feet, take his mug back to the kitchen to rinse it, put on his coat and leave. As he walked towards the exit he nodded at Liv.

"Have a nice evening," he said.

LIV GOT HOME LATE THAT NIGHT. There was something wrong with her bike and it took ages to cycle up the hill to her flat. Liv had lived in the same flat for six years with her friend Julie. Liv knew Julie better than anyone, including Julie herself. For instance, Liv knew that Julie's walk was completely silent; that however firmly Julie placed her feet on the floor, the ground rose up to meet them, cushioning their arrival and suffocating sound. Julie would have made an excellent spy and when they'd first moved in together— back when they were still trying to figure out what to do with their lives—Liv had spent hours trying to convince Julie to apply for MI5. "How about I fill in the details for you," Liv said, opening up the online form. Julie laughed and told Liv she was mad. Liv soon got cross and started filling out the form anyway until she came to a space for a bit of information about Julie that she didn't know. By this point Julie had scuttled off to the kitchen.

"You simply have to join MI5," Liv said when she found her. "For our safety."

"I do have an interview tomorrow," Julie said.

"With who?"

"Another consultancy."

Eventually one of the consultancy firms gave Julie a job. They didn't know that by employing her they were depriving the nation of probably its best ever spy.

Liv sometimes took comfort in the fact that if Julie was actually a spy she would not be allowed to tell people. Every time Julie was vague about what exactly she did for the consultancy, Liv reassured herself that the whole consultancy thing was a façade and that Julie was in fact desperately collecting information on unknown threats. Most likely MI5 got bored waiting for her to apply and headhunted her. Headhunting did happen. Liv knew this for a fact. Apparently Julie was headhunted by her current consultancy.

A year or so earlier, because she was so tired from being a spy at the same time as working for the consultancy, Julie had allowed herself to be seduced by a vastly inferior man called Roy. Roy's arms seemed to be permanently attached to Julie and when they weren't touching her they were hanging limp in the room like clothes left to dry on a line. When Liv got back from work she found Julie and Roy in the kitchen, tittering over a pan of tomato sauce. Liv had wanted to talk to Julie about the fact that the unsuccessful candidate from the interviews a week earlier had spent the whole day sat in the office, but instead she ended up watching Roy clasp himself to Julie's legs as they tried to eat pasta for dinner.

THE NEXT DAY Liv was late for work. The problem with the bike turned out to be a slow puncture and halfway to the office the back tyre was flat on the tarmac. Liv chained the bike to a sturdy looking railing and got the bus instead. It was packed and Liv was squeezed up against the window for the rest of her journey. She arrived in the office feeling sweaty and unpleasant.

The unsuccessful candidate was already at the spark desk. He was just as freshly presented as he had been at his interview. He sat up straight, a mug of steaming coffee on a coaster beside him. He appeared to be trying to log on to the computer. As Liv sat down, the unsuccessful candidate turned around.

"Morning," he said with a grin.

At lunch on their way to get sandwiches, Fran asked how the new guy was getting on.

"You mean Liam?" Liv said.

"No, the other one," Fran said. "The one they employed to replace Ben."

"That's Liam," said Liv. "I've no idea who the other guy is?"

"He must be from the Birmingham office."

"He's not," Liv said. "He was at the interviews. I remember seeing him waiting outside Jane's office, but he didn't get the job. Liam did."

"Liam can be quite annoying," Fran said.

"Should I call Jane?" Liv asked.

Fran shrugged. "I heard she's super busy at the moment with the restructuring at the Birmingham office. Maybe just drop her an email to let her know what's going on. If it's an issue then at least you've covered your back."

That afternoon, as the unsuccessful candidate took paperwork from one of the drawers and arranged it in piles on the desk, Liv wrote an email to Jane. She explained that someone had been sitting at the spare desk beside Liam since Monday and that she thought Jane ought to know. Liv added a sentence to explain how she was almost certain that the man sitting at the desk was the unsuccessful candidate from the interviews now more than a week earlier, but that looked weird so she deleted it before she hit send.

Around three, the unsuccessful candidate turned from the documents on his desk.

"Already drowning in paperwork," he said with a grin.

On the way home, Liv got a text from Julie to ask if they could meet in the pub. It sounded urgent so Liv left her bike chained to the railing and took the bus all the way up the hill. When she got to the pub, Julie announced that she was going to move out and into a house Roy had bought with an inheritance from his grandma.

"This is a bad idea," Liv said. "Won't you want your own space?"

Roy was at the bar paying for drinks but somehow still had a hand hovering behind Julie's head.

"Look," said Julie. "I know this isn't ideal for you, but I'll help find someone to take my room. Can you please be happy for me?"

"I'm delighted for you," Liv said.

Roy returned from the bar, hauling himself back to the table by clinging onto Julie's shoulder and dragging his expensive loafers across the pub's fake parquet floor.

"This pub's actually got a surprisingly good beer list," he said.

"It's not surprising," Liv said. "It's gentrification."

"How's work?" Julie asked.

Liv thought about the unsuccessful candidate who had now shown up at the office two days in a row, but she was cross with Julie for moving out so she just said everything was fine. Julie went to stay at Roy's that night so Liv finished her beer and went home to eat leftover pasta. Afterwards, she lay in bed reading an article about famous twentieth century dictators until at some point she fell asleep.

On Wednesday Liv got in to find the desk next to Liam empty and an email from Jane that said she was going to be tied up in Birmingham for the rest of the week. There was no mention of the unsuccessful candidate or anyone else who might be using the spare desk in the meantime. When Fran arrived she pointed to the empty desk and gave Liv a thumbs-up.

The unsuccessful candidate showed up at ten past nine.

"Sorry I'm late," he said as he removed his coat and sat down. He wore the same grey suit he'd worn on each occasion Liv had seen him, but today he had on a blue shirt and a bright yellow tie. He started tapping at the keyboard as he turned on the computer.

"Emails," he said as Liv got up to get coffee. "They just pile up don't they."

While Liv waited for the coffee to percolate she tried her best to remain calm. Don't be silly, she told herself, there must be a plausible explanation. She could hear Mr. Daniels on the floor of the office, murmuring something to Liam, so he must've been able to see the unsuccessful candidate right beside him at the spare desk. Wouldn't he have something to say? Soon, though, Liv saw Mr. Daniels march back past the kitchen to the conference room. There was no suggestion that anything was amiss.

By the time the coffee was ready, Liv felt slightly better. Whoever the newcomer was, he must be a different guy. She'd only seen the final two candidates for a few minutes while they waited to be interviewed. It probably *was* someone from the Birmingham office, moved here as part of the restructuring. Plus she hadn't slept well and she knew she was addled from the shock of Julie moving out. Her wits weren't at their sharpest.

Back at the desk the unsuccessful candidate still hadn't managed to log on and had returned to his piles of paper. Liam was on the phone talking to someone in the Birmingham office about a game involving West Ham and Aston Villa. Fran was asking Liv if she could email her a copy of the form you used to request leave. The unsuccessful candidate started drinking from a bottle of water. He held a gulp in his mouth for a few moments as he stared out across the office, before he swallowed and swung his chair back round towards the desk.

That weekend, Julie insisted she and Liv have lunch at a new food market that had opened up at the bottom of the hill.

"They do great wraps," Julie said. "You'll love them."

"Will I?" Liv said.

"Roy says they're exceptional," Julie said.

Under pressure, Liv selected a carrot and tofu wrap with a peanut sauce. Julie, on Roy's recommendation, went for pistachio hummus with roasted courgette and cranberries. As they ate, Julie explained that she'd just started a new project working for a different company through the same consultancy, which Liv realised meant she must have started a new undercover operation.

"Is it dangerous?" Liv asked.

"Not really," Julie said. "We're only there to address a few key issues."

"What kind of key issues."

"All sorts. Often it's a question of identity or communication. Sometimes an old-fashioned way of thinking has become entrenched and is blocking new ways of thinking. It's about opening up a space to reflect."

"Kind of like a therapist?"

"Kind of," Julie said. "What have you been up to?"

"I've been reading a lot about dictators. Isn't it weird how all the dictators that were in power when we were kids aren't in power anymore? Saddam Hussein, Slobodan Milošević, Colonel Gaddafi, Kim Jong-Il."

"Didn't he die?"

"Most of them died. The point is suddenly there seems to be no more dictators and while I'm sure that's a good thing it also feels like a big change."

"How's work."

"Robert Mugabe as well."

"Are you still applying for other jobs?"

"Although I can never remember if he's still in power."

When they finished their wraps, Julie went to Roy's sister's birthday party and Liv went to pick up her bike. When she got back to the railing she realised she'd forgotten the keys to the lock.

THE FOLLOWING MONDAY, Liv got an email from Jane to say she'd be stuck in the Birmingham office for at least another fortnight. She thanked Liv for taking care of Liam and said the accounts team should go out to lunch to get to know one another. "Keep the receipts," Jane wrote. "I'll reimburse."

After consulting with Fran, Liv decided to take Liam to the café a couple of streets away where they did baked potatoes. As they were leaving, Liv spotted the unsuccessful candidate still sat at the spare desk. He was wearing a new pale apricot shirt today and was drinking coffee as he examined a ledger.

"Some of us are going to this café for lunch," Liv said. "They do a half-decent baked potato."

The unsuccessful candidate looked a little startled. Liv noticed a lunchbox on the table beside him with some sandwiches on wholemeal bread.

"It's okay if you've got your lunch," Liv said.

"No," the unsuccessful candidate replied firmly. "No, I'll come. I can always eat these for dinner."

At the café they ordered potatoes with chilli con carne and cheese and listened to Liam talk about a trip he'd taken to Tallinn for his friend Dean's stag do.

"Whole thing was epic," he explained. "Four days. Eight blokes. One eastern European capital. You do the maths."

There was silence amidst the steaming potatoes.

"Carnage?" the unsuccessful candidate eventually said.

"Exactly," Liam said, slapping him across the back. "Total carnage. Have you been to Estonia?"

"Not recently," the unsuccessful candidate said softly.

For a moment Liv wondered if now was a good time to ask who the unsuccessful candidate was and why he was showing up to the office every day. Before she could speak, though, Liam was off again. While they finished their potatoes they listened to him describe the moment Dean threw up in an Estonian taxi as the single funniest moment of his entire life. The unsuccessful candidate spent the whole meal listening intently and smiling wistfully to himself.

"Do you live nearby?" Liv asked the unsuccessful candidate on the walk back to the office.

He looked up, his eyes steady in his round face. Liv noticed that he'd cut himself shaving, a nick on one side of his throat. It was the first blemish she'd noticed in his otherwise immaculate appearance.

"Not far," he said.

Back at the office Liv watched the unsuccessful candidate return to his desk. For a while he went through paperwork, but he soon tired and ended up just sitting there staring at the login screen on the computer. At around half-two he got up and asked if anyone wanted coffee.

"My man," Liam said.

For the rest of the week, Liv watched the unsuccessful candidate show up every day. He made coffee in the kitchen, took scrap paper to recycling and made notes in the ledger he'd found in the drawer. He was always perfectly presented, save for the shaving cut, which slowly started to scab over and left a mark on his skin. Sometimes he would come to lunch with them at the café, other times he would eat homemade sandwiches at the desk. Most of the time he just sat in the chair and stared at the blank monitor. He would wait for the screen to shut down and then nudge the mouse to bring it back to life.

On Friday they all went to the pub after work. The unsuccessful candidate bought a round of drinks and as they gathered at the bar he raised a glass and said how welcome he'd been made to feel and how much he enjoyed being part of the team. Later, in the toilets, Liv confronted Fran.

"I mean should he even be here?" she said. "Should I not tell Jane."

"Liam is actually a complete knob," Fran said. "If I have to hear about that fucking stag do one more time I swear I'm going to—"

"I'm not talking about Liam," Liv said. "I'm talking about the other guy."

"He's unbearable. I don't know how you put up with him. If it was me I'd be talking to Jane and asking to move desks."

"So I should tell Jane?" Liv said plaintively.

Fran shrugged and said she was heading home. Liv would have gone home too, but Julie was visiting Roy's parents and she didn't want to sit in an empty flat all evening by herself. She went with Liam and the unsuccessful candidate to another bar where Liam made them all do shots and was astonished to learn that Liv had never seen *Die Hard*.

"Why would I have seen *Die Hard*?"

"Because you're human and alive. What films do you like?"

"Often I read," said Liv.

"Well what do you read?"

"I just finished a book about the history of the Balkan states."

"I read a history book recently, about World War II," Liam said.

"That's not history," Liv said. "That's just stuff that happened while our grandparents were alive that everyone uses to justify certain truths."

Liam looked slightly confused. "You've seen *Die Hard*, right?" he said to the unsuccessful candidate.

The unsuccessful candidate confirmed that he had indeed seen *Die Hard*. Later Liam fell over in the toilets and the unsuccessful candidate took him home in a cab.

"You can jump in if you want," he told Liv. "We can drop you off on the way?"

"I'm fine," Liv said.

"This man's a legend," Liam slurred.

On the bus home, Liv remembered that her bike was still attached to the railing at the bottom of the hill.

That Sunday, Liv went with Julie to look at the house she and Roy had bought. Everything smelled of paint and there was a breakfast bar that Roy was apparently delighted with. "It's a life's ambition," Julie said. Afterwards they went for coffee in a café that had planks of wood screwed to the walls instead of wallpaper. The drinks were served by a young man in a tracksuit and wireframed glasses who used the word *you* a lot. "You want your coffees," he said. "You want your lattes? You want something to eat?" The coffee was actually exceptionally good.

"I'm going to help you find a new flatmate," Julie said.

"Aren't you busy with the new house and the consulting and being a spy?"

"Not so busy I can't put an ad on Spareroom and help you meet a few potentials."

"I was thinking I might try living on my own for a while."

"I can easily ask a few people at work."

"I think when you're twenty-nine you're not meant to be still living with flatmates. It's partners or by yourself. Them's the rules."

Back in the flat, they did a tally and worked out that apart from the futon Liv slept on and a few books, pretty much everything belonged to Julie. Once the sofa and coffee table and TV were gone and most of the pots and pans were out of the kitchen, hardly anything was going to be left.

"At least let me give you the sofa," Julie said. "I'll feel bad if I leave the place empty. Besides, Roy's very particular about furniture so I expect we'll get a lot of things new."

Liv told Julie not to be so dramatic. "I like minimalism," she explained. "Always have."

As Julie started sorting out her room, Liv found herself thinking about the unsuccessful candidate. He'd shown up in the office every day for almost a month now. All he did was sit at his desk all day, fiddling with the computer and drinking coffee. Yet no-one else seemed to have noticed. Ever since he'd arrived the whole office had just carried on as normal around him without the slightest hint that anything was amiss. It was because Jane was away. Everything was bound to get sorted once she got back.

TWO WEEKS LATER, Liv got an email from Jane to say that she was going to be stuck in the Birmingham office for at least another month. She thanked Liv for looking after Liam and hoped he was settling in okay. Liv drafted a reply in which she explained that Liam seemed to be settling in just fine, but that the unsuccessful candidate from the interviews was still showing up in the office every day. He was there as Liv wrote the email, stood by the spare desk to unbutton his coat.

"Coffee anyone?" he said as he made his way to the kitchen.

Liv nodded and deleted the second half of the email. When the unsuccessful candidate got back with the coffees she gave him her login details and showed him how to get into the accounts system. She assigned him some of her accounts and some of the accounts she was planning to pass on to Liam. For the rest of the month the unsuccessful candidate sat at the desk, diligently going through paperwork, checking for outstanding orders and contacting the clients purchasing department when required. By the end of the month all the accounts were up to date and the unsuccessful candidate had started clearing out the redundant files in the system.

"You really don't have to do that," Liv said. "It's a pretty thankless task."

The unsuccessful candidate smiled. "It's no bother," he replied.

On the way home that night, Liv got off the bus at the bottom of the hill and finally went to pick up her bike. Someone had stolen the front wheel and the lock was so badly rusted that however much Liv jiggled the key it refused to budge. Frustrated, Liv took a step back only to realise that she had the wrong bike. For the next hour she wandered around all the railings in the area looking for the right one. She couldn't find it. In the end she gave in and walked back up the hill.

The flat was empty when Liv got home and she remembered that Julie had planned to pick up the last of her stuff that day. Although Julie'd been spending most of her time in her new house anyway, her books and clothes and poster of the cover of *Lady Chatterley's Lover* no longer being in the flat somehow felt definite. It wasn't so much to do with the things that were not in the flat and more to do with the things that still were. For a long time Liv stared at her reflection in the oven door. Then she made herself beans on toast and read about Robert Mugabe online.

The following Tuesday, Mr. Daniels ambled over to say that he was taking the whole of the accounts team out to lunch. At half-twelve Liv, Fran, Liam, and the unsuccessful candidate all made their way down to the bistro where Mr. Daniels was on high-five terms with the staff.

"Jane tells me you guys have been holding the whole thing together," Mr. Daniels said as they looked at the menus. "So order whatever you want."

Liam and Mr. Daniels ordered pig cheeks in red-wine sauce. Fran had an asparagus quiche. Liv and the unsuccessful candidate both ordered pollack with a pine nut crust.

As Liv nibbled frantically at the nutty fish skin, she felt herself waiting for the moment when Mr. Daniels would turn to the un-successful candidate and ask him who the hell he was and what the hell he was doing there. Instead, the two of them talked calmly about one of the Birmingham accounts that had been transferred and, over coffee, a beach in Cornwall where they'd both been on holiday as kids. Liv noticed that the unsuccessful candidate's scab had peeled away to leave a small scar on his throat, which rotated slightly as he ate his apple crumble for dessert.

"Can you excuse me," Liv said suddenly, jerking back from the table and marching outside. She stood there in the street, by the bistro window, pacing up and down in the cold.

Eventually Fran came to find her. "Is everything all right?" she asked.

"I lost my bike," Liv explained, shivering. "I chained it up somewhere and now I can't find it."

"Someone probably stole it," Fran said.

"I'm pretty sure I just forgot where I put it."

"Even with a lock it makes no difference. They come with a van and scoop it up."

"I just lost it," Liv said.

On the walk back to the office, Liam tried to arrange an evening where they all met up to watch *Die Hard*.

"Liv's never seen it," he said. "Can you believe it?"

Everyone, including the unsuccessful candidate, laughed.

IN EARLY DECEMBER, Liv went to Julie and Roy's housewarming party. It wasn't like any house party Julie had ever had in the flat with Liv. Roy's sister was there with her husband and a two-year-old that kept asking everyone their name.

"I'm Liv," said Liv.

"Olive?"

"No, just Liv."

"Try Olivia," said Roy.

"No," said Liv. "Try Liv."

The child started screaming and ran in search of a parent.

"Is there anything to drink?" Liv asked.

"Julie got given some nice wine by a client," Roy said.

"What about gin?"

Roy looked bewildered. Liv tracked down Julie who found her some gin in the back of a cupboard. Liv took her gin to the patio because Julie said Roy wouldn't like it if she smoked inside. Julie came out with her.

"What have you been up to?"

"I've been reading about Saddam Hussein," said Liv. "He was truly a terrible man. It's probably good that he's not in power. I know America messed Iraq up, but if you're such a bad man you shouldn't be allowed to run a country."

Julie said it was probably more complicated than that.

"What are you spying on at the moment?" Liv asked.

"How many times do I have to tell you I'm not a spy," Julie laughed.

"Oh yeah, of course. What are you consulting at the moment?"

Julie said she was helping a telecoms business with communication. Liv nodded and listened diligently. She left after the second gin. On the bus home she saw her bike chained to a railing on the opposite side of the road but by the time she rang the bell the bus was well past it.

TWO WEEKS LATER the whole office went bowling for the staff Christmas party. With Jane still in Birmingham, Liam had volunteered to organise it. For a flat rate you got a Mexican meal, three pitchers of beer, and unlimited bowl. By nine everyone was shaky on their bowling shoes and a game had been organised between accounts and IT. Liv was surprised at how everyone seemed able to step up and hurl the enormously heavy balls down the wooden floor in a way that sent the pins tumbling every time. Whenever Liv let go of the ball it would dribble to one side and flop unceremoniously into the gutter. Eventually, she just gave up and went and sat on a bench.

"Are you not bowling," said the unsuccessful candidate as he sat down beside Liv and poured them each a beer from a pitcher.

"I can't do it," Liv said. "What's your excuse?"

"Apparently they couldn't find me in the system," he said.

Liv stared at Liam and Fran who were cheering as Keith from IT prepared to bowl.

"Do you ever feel as though nothing you do is actually happening?" Liv said. "As if everything is happening around you and you can't do anything to stop it?"

The unsuccessful candidate took a sip of his beer. "I used to," he said. "I used to feel that nothing I did really mattered to anyone."

"What changed?" Liv asked.

"Nothing," the unsuccessful candidate said. "But you just keep going, don't you? You keep going through the motions until it matters again."

A little later, Liam came over and said that Fran was too drunk to finish her round so they needed a volunteer to complete it.

"Who?" Liv asked.

"Anyone," Liam shrugged. "Doesn't matter who, but we're in the middle of a game so until someone steps up everyone's just stood round doing nothing."

The unsuccessful candidate took a sip from his beer. Liv noticed that the scar on his throat had faded away to nothing, as if it had never been there in the first place.

"You go," she said to him. "I'm really not very good."

The unsuccessful candidate beamed at her. He looked delighted as he put down his pint and strode up to the lane in his smart brown shoes. He was still wearing the same grey suit he'd worn on the day of the interview, but he moved easily beneath it. His limbs were strong and supple. Liv watched over his shoulder as he tried a few of the bowling balls for size, testing his fingers in the holes until he was happy that he'd found one that fitted. He seemed to know exactly what he was doing. There was an assurance to the way he lifted the ball to his chest. In a fluid movement he stepped forward, bent a knee, smoothly lowered his arm and released the ball.

As the ball spun down the lane, the unsuccessful candidate held his pose: knee on the ground, fingertips almost caressing the varnished wood. His eyes were fixed on the tight rows of black and white pins the ball was bearing down on. Liv remembered how, when she'd first seen the unsuccessful candidate on the day of his interview, he'd seemed far too sharply dressed to work in accounts. Kneeling there with his back to her, the clean lines of his grey suit and the elegance of his brown shoes still appeared at odds with the mass of white shirts and black trousers that she now noticed were gathered around the end of the lane to see where the ball would end up.

The ball swirled across the wood, spinning and turning as it rushed away from the crowd. At first it appeared to be veering off to the right and into the gutter, but as it rolled on it began to curve, angling back across the lane towards the pins. People continued to edge forward. Liv saw them converge at the edges of her vision, encroaching on the unsuccessful candidate like a crowd through a turnstile. Fran was dragging herself to her feet. Liam was bending at the waist to squint down the lane at the pins. Mr. Daniels appeared, too, moving across Liv's line of sight to stand directly between her and the unsuccessful candidate who was still knelt on the floor. They pressed in around him, closer and closer, tighter and tighter still, until, before Liv could see whether the ball would topple the pins, the unsuccessful candidate was swallowed by the crowd and disappeared from sight.

*from*

# Politics

DAVID KILLED THE QUEEN. It was nothing personal, he said. It was just politics. All he wanted was to make a political statement about the abuse of power in the country. After consideration, David had decided that power must be approached on its own terms. The terms of power—as everyone knows—finally reduce to violence, so David shot the Queen in the back of the head from near enough point blank range. Above all David did not want to waste lives unnecessarily—violence can take indiscriminate forms—but killing the Queen, he argued, was a symbolic gesture. Besides, she was old. "Truth be told," he said, "she didn't even know who I was."

THE MEDIA OF COURSE WERE NOT CONTENT with the cut of David's politics. They painted his grievances with the Queen as exclusively personal. He loathed the Queen, they wrote, he would vomit on stamps and pinned up over the walls of his room were images in which he had cut out her eyes.

"She's a symbol! She's a cipher!" David told the arresting officer. "She *represents!* All I want is a more representative democracy with a more accountable head of state."

"Is this about proportional representation?" asked the officer.

"Damn right it's about proportional representation," said David. "It's about us as citizens having our voices heard."

Fragments of David's statement were leaked to the press, twisted horribly and printed alongside an artist's impression of the contents of his hard drive.

"What David forgets," said an increasingly popular MP, "is that in this country we are not citizens but subjects."

DAVID'S CLASSMATES WERE UNANIMOUSLY SHOCKED. The Queen had only been visiting their school to open a new science department and at that point few people knew anything about David's politics. No-one expected him to step out of the line of spectators. No-one ever imagined he'd have a gun. "He couldn't even bloody catch," said a Geography teacher, who once took David for cricket.

One by one his peers were taken in for questioning.

"We got off once," Kayleigh confessed. "On the coach on the way back from Germany. We weren't close though. In fact, I hardly knew him at all. But I needed to get back at my ex for being such a dick in Berlin."

"Nothing in his character to suggest he was born to kill?"

"On the coach he was playing *Grand Theft Auto* on his phone?"

Kayleigh was let off with a warning and urged to think carefully before launching into relationships with compromising men.

For History and Politics, David had sat beside a boy called Charles. "I wouldn't say we got on," Charles explained. "You see I, like most sensible people, believe in the benefits of free market capitalism. I think it's the state that should be shrunk if enterprise is not to suffocate. I remain unconvinced about the long-term funding options for a National Health Service and I enjoy reading the novels of Ayn Rand. David, though, was, you know, a bit..."

"A bit?"

"You know, one of..."

"One of what?"

"One of them."

"I'M NOT A SOCIALIST or a communist or an anarchist. I do not want a revolution on any scale. I simply want a democratic government and an elected head of state."

"We have it on good authority that you've been reading the works of Karl Marx."

"Who told you that?"

"We can't say."

"Was it Charles? Because if anyone needs locking up, it's Charles. He thinks wealth trickles down. He knows all the verses of the national anthem. He sleeps beside a copy of *Atlas Shrugged*."

David was told that for all his sins Charles had not shot the Queen.

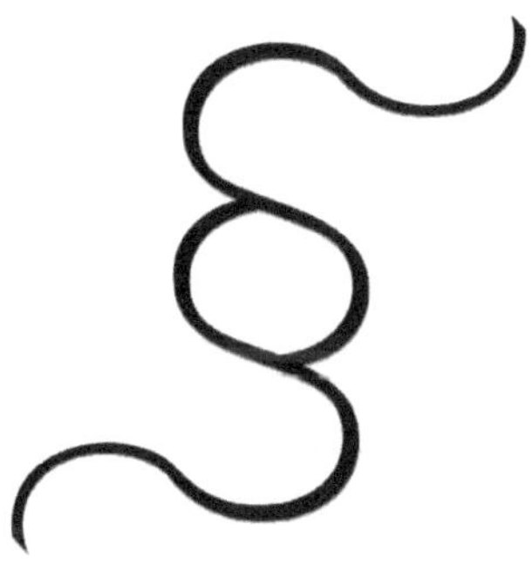

Thomas Chadwick's 'Politics'
is available in its entirety at
ThisIsSplice.co.uk/2019/04/15/politics

Victoria Manifold

# An Introduction to
# Victoria Manifold

Thomas Chadwick

DURING A RECORDING SESSION for their first album, producer Martin Hannett asked Joy Division to go for another take but this time play "slower but faster." This seemingly contradictory phrase was apparently normal for Hannett who, in the course of recording the album, would also demand that the drummer, Stephen Morris, reassemble his whole kit to eliminate a rattle that only Hannett could hear, as well as trying to capture a specific drum sound through a speaker perched on a toilet in the studio basement. The result of Hannett's instructions was the unique sound of *Unknown Pleasures*, but it's the seemingly implausible request to play "slower and faster" that I think can help formulate one of the tenets of good writing and why Victoria Manifold's work has it.

Another way of expressing "slower but faster" might be the creative writing school doctrine of "less is more." The problem with "less is more," though, is that it is all too often interpreted as meaning that more can be achieved simply by saying less. Understood in these dogmatic terms, "less is more" becomes an exercise in reduction not to minimalism itself but—worse—to minimal priorities, to taking things away until there is nothing that stands out. This is not a neutral point. As has recently been pointed out by Eric Bennett, less is more can actually be placed at the heart of the CIA's direct attempts to frame "good writing" in Cold War-era

America as work that contains "sensations, not doctrines; experiences, not dogmas; memories, not philosophies." Yet this is a lazy interpretation of "less is more" and one that Hannett's "slower but faster" helps to unlock. "Less is more" is not about paring down and reducing writing to sensations, experiences, and memories, but about generating more from those sensations, experiences, and memories than the reader might think. A good sentence is one greater than the sum of its parts, a sentence where less *is* more— one played slower but faster.

I first read Victoria Manifold when her story 'Clerical Error' was shortlisted for the *White Review* prize in 2016 and made available on the *White Review* website. The story is about a flatshare in which the current Prime Minister has ended up living in the boxroom of the narrator's house. "It's an awkward situation," the narrator discloses, "but we're trying to make the best of it." 'Clerical Error' is also a fine example of a piece of writing that expands outwards, constantly seeking to exceed the confines of the story itself. The Prime Minister, it turns out, is the least of the narrator's problems. At work her office is facing cuts and the threat of redundancy hovers in the air. At home her flatmates are equally difficult: a couple break up and continue to live in the same room; Karen thinks she and the narrator have developed a connection because their menstrual cycles have synced. Slowly it emerges that it is the narrator's fault that the Prime Minister is living in the boxroom and everyone—including the Prime Minister—starts to resent her for it. Events become more bizarre, but, within the confines the story has created for itself, no less plausible. The narrator fakes a report for her boss as the Prime Minister starts a war after a failed sporting fixture. In a couple of thousand words the reader is treated not only to the despair of a flatshare but also the pain of an entire nation.

What stands out about Victoria's writing is its capacity to wring more from a story than you as a reader ever thought could be in there. The writing is not overblown or grandiose, but it looms large with every sentence. Often the results are hilarious. Take *Columblog*, for instance: the blog on which Victoria has written about watching every episode of the American TV series *Columbo* over the course of two years. Her posts there are rarely more than a few hundred words long, but the writing is always drum tight and strangely addictive. Narratives emerge across posts, exceeding the confines of individual episodes, edging out from beyond the framework of the detective series itself.

'Whitegoods for Your Daughters' has exactly the quality of being "slower but faster" that is at the heart of all Victoria's work. The story is set during "funeral season" in Sydney and narrated by a recent divorcee who takes a job at Burns, Burns & Burns, one of twelve funeral homes on the "funeral strip." The scenario is at once wildly bizarre and painfully mundane, but it is presented so unapologetically that the reader has no choice but to follow the narrator along. She is thousands of miles from home and profoundly lonely, yet the story reaches beyond her circumstances to fixate on the loneliness that exists within the minutiae of all daily existence. There is, in the narrator, a yearning for intimacy from within routine. At one point she notes the small excitement of a mourner crying close enough for her to feel the heat of the tears. As is the case in 'Clerical Error,' the narrator appears to be on the edge of failure, but a perhaps bigger fear is that if and when she does fail, no-one will notice. The story takes the mundane and manages to make it both weird and familiar, generating an excess from this tension. It is less *and* more. It is slower but faster.

# Whitegoods for Your Daughters

During the height of funeral season I began working as a receptionist at Burns, Burns & Burns, the first funeral parlour along the Pymble funeral strip.

As it does every year, funeral season had taken the many funeral homes of Pymble by surprise and they desperately scrambled to hire the extra staff needed to get them through those months unscathed. They advertised on local television, in free newspapers, in newspapers you paid for, on sheets of coloured paper taped to lampposts, the bottom edges of which were cut in such a way that they fluttered in the hot wind, making it easy to tear off the telephone numbers printed on them. That year quite a few of them had also splurged on sky writers. Puffs of white against the painfully blue sky commanded those below to WORK IN FUNERALS NOW. Unfortunately, as further details on how to apply were not provided, it proved to be an expensive mistake for those investing in this particular method of recruitment.

I had read the writing looming in the sky above me. I had watched the garish commercials on my local television. And I had torn off the strips of paper from the lampposts and studied them as if they were ancient hieroglyphs. The names were attractive and plentiful: Elegant Funeral Designs, Tru Pro Funerals, Executive Funeral Ambition, White Lady Funerals, John's Funerals, Cut Price Funeral Dread, and, of course, Burns, Burns & Burns.

My position there had been created solely to meet the demands of the season, to greet the sweat-soaked mourners, almost entirely spent from the heat and grief, and to occupy them in a superficial manner whilst more important business was conducted beyond the curtain hanging behind my desk. Business more definite and purposeful than my own, requiring specialised tools and knowledge, hard to acquire chemicals and clothes with an unusual fit—trousers too tight around the thighs but baggy at the knees, calves, and ankles; a jacket almost comically big in the shoulders but resisting all attempts to be buttoned up around the middle.

The job had become an inconvenient necessity to me as I emerged dull and ragged from my first divorce, a costly enterprise that had left me needing money quickly. I had naturally assumed that further divorces were to follow; after all, I was still young enough and talented enough to dissolve perhaps five or more marriages before I tired of the process. So I had shed my winter clothes and shoes, my husband and the veneer of stability I had worked so hard to sustain. Now I sweated through loose cotton dresses and bought coffee at the 7-Eleven, counting out pocketfuls of twenty-cent coins and hoping the night manager there might ask me to marry him so I could begin it all over again.

Of course I was looking for anything that might quell the little frights that bubbled up inside me sometimes. I was looking for a way to stop myself reconstructing the minutiae of every moment of the last eighteen months, playing out scene after scene from my decaying marriage until I was exhausted. I was looking for a way to stop myself from picturing my first ex-husband's face every time I masturbated, and a way to stop using the language we had invented together in secret—that sort of pathetically ordinary thing that couples sometimes do but that was still so painful to me.

I was always empty and full at the same time, sustaining myself on cheap foods and a peculiar strain of homesickness. My first ex-husband lived ten thousand miles from where I was born and now I did too. I couldn't afford the airfare home and even if I could've I hated to return stinking of failure as badly as I did now. This homesickness had grown to be a hard ball that sat on the top of my stomach, under my ribs. I carried it with me everywhere and I luxuriated in it often: a specific kind of pain, sharply felt but edged with a woolly nostalgia. I tried to soften it by finding similarities between where I was and where I had come from. The smoke billowing from the chimneys of the ham processing factory could, in the right circumstances, be mistaken for the dense fog of the moors I ran across as a child. As long as I couldn't hear their voices, the men crowding into the RSL on Fridays and Saturdays could be the same ones who'd deliberately squeezed too close to me in the sticky pubs of my adolescence. And although the MSG broth sitting at the bottom of the polystyrene cups of noodles I ate didn't taste remotely like the thin stews my mother would make when I was growing up, it did have the same smell of poverty and desperation and, in that way, I could feel closer to home.

But in the end it was better to forget about home. Thinking about the distance only caused me to lose my breath and narrow my vision with a kind of vertiginous nausea. I imagined the effort needed to claw myself back to where I'd begun and those little frights exploded one after the other until I couldn't lift my arms or legs or eyelids. So it was best to think only of the immediate future—what time to set my alarm for, what to eat for lunch, how to interact with the other people who worked at Burns, Burns & Burns and, every day, how I might meet my next ex-husband.

At Burns, Burns & Burns I was needed to answer the phone, greet the real-life mourners who frequented the premises, do very basic things with a computer. It was the sort of low-level administration that had become a constant of my professional life and I was just about good enough at the job that no-one could tell how bad I was at it. I would sit at my desk just staring at my phone, creating complicated equations from the digits of my first ex-husband's phone number, and I'd leave the mourners to navigate their grief without my assistance. And if Mr. Roberts, the chief undertaker, came by, I would give him a look that said something like: *oh, this one is demented with grief; don't listen if she complains about the service.*

I was never reprimanded for my questionable work ethic. I liked to pretend I was fragile, or at least fragility seemed to seep from my body or radiate from my skin. "Don't raise your voice at me," I warned the world through my posture, my demeanour: "you might make me cry and then you'll feel uncomfortable." I didn't speak the words but I felt them flow from me in the angle of my smile, the way I positioned my hands or very slightly parted my lips, and the fragility I exuded seemed to grant me a certain kind of invisibility which, I admit, was often useful.

The hot, bright days of funeral season continued in this way. Working. Sweating. Keeping to myself. Moving slowly through the humidity, unable to look at anything directly. My eyes throbbing and painful, my skin swampy and pale. Some excitement when an attractive mourner cried in my vicinity, close enough to feel the heat from their tears. Little frights bursting in my chest when I thought about how I might only ever have one ex-husband.

I plodded through the routine duties of my days, a decent facsimile of a funeral parlour receptionist. I would say things like "oh yes, I'm up to my eyes today" or "ooh, one sec Donna I just need to quickly finish this" or "yep yep, snowed under" to make the performance seem more realistic. No-one around me could see the imitation for what it was, and every time, as they answered my comments with "never mind, it'll be the weekend soon!" or "we made it past hump day!" I felt myself getting both stronger and further away from them.

I half-heartedly tried to make friends with my colleagues, not in any sort of meaningful way but only so I didn't appear surly or totally unlovable. I ate the communal snacks that Mr. Roberts brought in, even if he bought Jatz or Shapes, which, despite their blandness, made my stomach swell painfully. I asked Donna about her children, although they seemed to me unusually uninteresting. Both were that pale, blonde genre of child with skin almost see-through and a dark, sickly look around the eyes. No eyebrows. I borrowed a DVD of a schlocky thriller about a man with multiple personality disorder from Faye, although I actively did not want to see it and also I didn't have a DVD player. I kept the DVD for what I felt was an appropriate number of days on the bedside table of the small room I rented in a share house and I then returned it to her, quoting the plot summary from Wikipedia and hurrying away before she could ask me any questions, such as "what was your favourite part of the schlocky thriller about a man with multiple personality disorder?" or "which actor's performance impressed you in the schlocky thriller about a man with multiple personality disorder?" When Denis described the Pymble strip as long and thin, easy to navigate but somehow unsatisfying, I bit my tongue instead of saying "just like my ex-husband's penis," as they seemed like the sort of people who would consider such an observation vulgar, singling me out as unprofessional and risking the fragile invisibility I'd somehow constructed around myself.

Sometimes I went for lunch with Bronwyn, the receptionist at Executive Funeral Ambition. We had met some months earlier on the bus to Pymble, both clutching those paper strips we'd torn from lampposts. It was humiliating for both us to be on the bus. Public transport is great, of course it is, but there's no denying there's something undignified in it. Especially in this place, where the heat incubates a very particular sickness, fogging up the windows with it. Everything that seeps from the bodies of the other passengers turns into a thick gas and you're trapped in there, chewing on it without choice, feeling it settle on the surface of your skin without the means or opportunity to wash it off.

As I took a seat beside her, our eyes meeting and locking then shifting perceptibly down to each other's paper strips, there was a tense feeling, something akin to rivalry. But it soon dissolved when Bronwyn and I realised that we'd both have jobs at funeral parlours by the end of the day. After that we met once a week, pretending a friendship by walking a few metres to the pub on the corner and ordering $9 chicken schnitzels with your choice of hot chips and salad or veg and mash. It was a good deal and we ate greedily, as if we did work that required a level of energy such a meal provided instead of largely sedentary desk jobs that expended the very minimum of physical and mental power.

Outside, the air was always hot and thick and even when a tropical storm hit the Pymble strip I found it difficult to breathe properly. What afflicted me seemed to be something more than just the respiratory problems associated with my childhood poverty. It felt as if the very air of the place knew I was an interloper and was doing its best to suffocate me.

At the height of one storm, we sat under an inadequate awning and ate the schnitties and hot chips. Bronwyn's bit of salad blew away and I watched it flap into a gutter puddle as she told me about the time she went to a music festival in a desert and burned effigies at sunset. I pulled the hood of my raincoat tightly around my face as hot wind lashed us and I felt absolutely fevered, choked.

Sweat stuck my raincoat to my skin. I said, "Your festival sounds good." But I didn't mean it.

When humidity reached 95% everything seemed to expand in the hot damp air: leaves grew to the size of shed roofs, cockroaches were these long fat swellings of shiny brown on the bathroom walls and kitchen floor. My body got bigger too. The tops of my thighs rubbed together and became sore. Red stretchmarks appeared on my stomach. They expanded downward into my pubic hair and I traced my fingers over the angry lines as I lay naked in bed, trying to keep cool. Even my hair seemed to grow faster, trapping wet heat at the back of my neck and making the collars of my clothes foetid.

Everything got hotter and damper and bigger until one day a man in an impeccable ute pulled up and asked if we'd like to buy any whitegoods. "They make excellent gifts," he said, "for all your family. Whitegoods for your daughters." Mr. Roberts, having sired only sons, lost interest quickly. Donna didn't spend any money without consulting her husband first and Faye and Denis and all the others didn't seem to want whitegoods, although they appeared near new and were being sold for an unbeatable price.

The Burns, Burns & Burns air conditioning unit had been broken for some time and every day a pool of sweat gathered in the waistband of my knickers. The man with the ute didn't have a replacement AC but suggested a minifridge I could plug in under my desk. It was good to think about having the fridge there, where no-one could see it, opening it up and putting my feet inside like I was in charge of everything. I gave him $30 for it and he asked me what it's like working at a funeral parlour. "It's okay," I said. But I could tell he wanted more than this. He wanted the dirty morbid details of death, maybe a murder or a mix-up with the bodies. Unfortunately for him, there was nothing like that at Burns, Burns & Burns. Further up the coast men took hatchets to their wives, and children were boiled alive in spa baths, but there it was calm and orderly and all the mess had been washed away, swept and tidied. Mr. Roberts' ethical crematorium, built from sustainable materials, was always hidden behind the heavy curtain. I'd never even seen a dead body. In fact my workplace was an utterly bloodless environment. There were tears, yes of course, floods of tears every day. Pale blank faces with eyes ringed in red, mouths always hanging open in shock or lips quivering involuntarily, but nothing you could describe as gory. All I could really tell the man were stories of the admittedly quotidian turf wars that arise when twelve funeral homes all set up shop along the same small stretch of streetside real estate. He seemed to be interested in this but I could tell his interest was feigned and I liked that about him.

Later that night, in the immaculate ute he'd bought the previous year from a private seller in Cessnock, he flicked his tongue over my clitoris and it felt good. So good I forgot the smell of myself, the heat of myself. He moved his head up, running his tongue and lips over my soft fat belly and the palms of his hands quickly over my nipples. "Is this okay?" he asked and I knew it was a question directed at me but somehow I kept forgetting to answer.

He started to visit Burns, Burns & Burns daily to check on the minifridge and every night he took me out to fuck me. We rode around in his still impeccable ute listening to those bands where a man sings "blah blah blah" sadly over and over until you just about fall asleep with the dirge of it. We drove past giant faded ads for long forgotten brands of shampoo and I pulled at the ends of my own dry and damaged curls, embarrassed by my odour rubbing against the clean stiff seats. But with the windows down it didn't seem so bad. Everything felt as if it all fit together and made sense then: the temperature outside, the red swollen parts of myself under my clothes, the sticky wet heat of my body and the hot damp mat of my hair. There seemed to be a reason for all of it.

There was something erotic in the way the man wore one sock bloodstained at the heel and one completely unstained sock. And when it got too hot he took off both socks and a caramel odour rose from his sweaty feet and hit us pleasantly. Then he'd turn up the sad man music and I'd smile at him as if I approved of it. We sped past brittle bouquets of flowers taped to the lamp-posts lining the roads. Little clouds of grief dust would spew from them with a small *poof* as we drove by. I'd look out the back and see the broken parts of petals and tissue paper settle on various marsupials smeared across the roads and I'd smile again but this time I'd make sure he couldn't see.

As the weeks went by we discovered the most comfortable way to fuck in a ute. He told me things about his life and I wondered how those things might impact me or how I could use them to push down all the little frights that so frequently bothered me. We drove past the house he grew up in, squat and dark, a single orange light illuminating his asthmatic mother. An inexplicably rusty pole stood firm against the hot wind on the front lawn. I asked him to find a graveyard but we drove for hours and still didn't see one. "It's the sort of thing you need to go out of state for," he told me.

It was during one of these drives that I saw a windsock for the first time. They don't really have them where I'm from, at least not that I can remember. It wasn't blowing about like I assumed it should but instead was pulled taut and still, suspended in the thick, warm air over the highway. He told me what it was and I repeated the word a few times, "windsock, windsock, windsock, windsock," whispering it like an incantation to protect me or a spell for some future success. We pulled over and I spent some time with his penis in my mouth, the tip all wet and hitting the back of my throat in a way I can only really describe as arousing.

When I was alone I would rehearse conversations with him, telling him how he would be my next ex-husband, how happy we would be for a short while, that we would remember each other fondly when we were old. These conversations always went well, and his answers always seemed to be exactly what I wanted to hear, so that when he came to take me out the next day I asked him to marry me.

He laughed at first, shook his head, asked if I was serious. I told him I was and I said we could always get divorced if he liked, and in fact I'd prefer it if we *did* get divorced at some point.

"The trouble is you're quite selfish."

This was not news to me.

"I mean, you don't even know my name. You didn't even ask my name."

That was true, but I really didn't think it was a reason not to marry me. It was just one of those details we could sort out later.

"And I told you I'm moving up to Queensland, weren't you listening?"

Of course I hadn't been listening but I tried to bluff my way through.

"Queensland, yes, plenty of daughters there."

"What?"

"For the whitegoods. To buy the whitegoods."

"Sure, yeah, if you like."

But he was on to me. He knew I saw him only as a minor character and he knew that, to me, everything that made up his life—the breathing machine his mother needed to stay alive, his tidy ute, the artificial pauses he inserted into most sentences, even the length and girth of his penis—could only ever be interesting asides in the much more interesting story of my life.

It was silent between us for a long time after that. The smears of light coming from the houses we passed made the roads seem very shiny, very wet. Eventually I heard that soft inhalation that means someone is about to speak and then I heard my heart in my chest.

"Should I just drop you at yours then?"

I nodded, remembering he was the person I was with when I'd first seen a windsock. It had only happened the night before, so, although it was a memory, it was a fresh one and I could be almost certain it hadn't been distorted yet. I felt bad. Not bad in the way I had felt when my first ex-husband told me I was too fat to cut my hair in a certain style. More like when my first ex-husband said I couldn't leave him until my depression was cured, as if that was a thing that happened to people.

"So what is your name?"

"Jared."

Jared, of course.

Jared didn't come around to check on the minifridge after that. By the following week the mourners had dwindled and the only work I had to do was reply to an email Denis had sent me asking about the intricacies of a PDF document. I accidentally spelled his name Denise and felt guilty about it when I bumped into him in the kitchenette. We shuffled awkwardly around the cutlery drawer and talked about the PDF some more. He gave me a double thumbs up but left a dirty mug in the sink, looking me straight in the eye as he set it down. I felt that any protection my fragility had given me had now been used up.

That evening, just before closing, Mr. Roberts handed me a thick white envelope but I didn't bother to open it. I knew what it would say. Everybody had stopped dying and they didn't need me anymore. Jared would be halfway to Queensland by now and I wasn't sure what do to with the minifridge. For the first time that year the wind felt cold and I made my hands into tight fists and put them in my pockets. When I took them out I had five twenty-cent coins in my palm. Exactly what I needed to get a coffee at the 7-Eleven near the bus stop. I could go there and smooth down my hair in a way that I imagined would impress the night manager. I could stop scratching at the spot my wedding band used to be in, but position my hand in such a way that you couldn't see the dry red skin circling my finger.

Waiting for the bus to arrive I chewed on the thin milky skin that had formed on top of the coffee. I could see the lights of the bus moving toward me from a distance but I couldn't quite make out the illuminated number on the front, maybe an eight, maybe a six. Finally the bus pulled up and I got on, unsure where it was going. I felt keenly the indignity of squeezing past the other passengers, my cheeks glowing a hot red. Bronwyn was sitting somewhere at the back but I pretended not to see her and chose a seat near the front, staring out the window at all the different lights and all the undertakers, *en masse*, walking steadily away from their places of work, a wave of awkward clothing choices pushing forward.

They were all my future ex-husbands beating a retreat from a life with me. Funeral season had drawn to a close and they'd emerged from under their hot lamps and dusty benches, discarding their ill-fitting suits and protective headgear. They wandered past the imposing towers of the ham processing factory, further and further back into the bush. I saw their silhouettes shrink as the Pymble strip darkened. You forget how beautiful it is sometimes, with the colour of the sky clear like it is and even at night the jacaranda trees so bright it hurts your eyes to look at them.

*from*

# The TV Show

ON THE WALL OF THE WARD, above our beds, there is one heavy and large-ish television BALANCED PRECARIOUSLY.

With nothing much else to do we have taken to watching the same TV show at the same time every day.

The TV show is perhaps seven or nine hours long but time works differently here so nothing is ever exact. The TV show is a quiz show with a high stakes element. The TV show could easily be described as a complex marathon. But the TV show could easily be described also as a discounted ballet or a rewarding balloon ride or a delicate professorial endeavour. That's the thing with using words to describe things—it's very easy to do.

I am injured in a secret way. And my arms, my arms are nothing special. Fingers at the ends, as expected. There are four other people on the ward with me and each of them has their own secret afflictions to incapacitate them. The doctors and nurses arrive on conveyor belts or mechanical trollies or those roller-skates they issue at the school for doctors and nurses and every day it is a different one, never the same medical practitioner twice. They touch us only when absolutely necessary.

Through a flap in the wall we are given our daily meal: dry flakes of sustainable fish in tins, lumps of wet custard in minia-ture polystyrene cauldrons. Although it is barely edible we take what is offered to us, but why wouldn't we? It's only natural.

Beneath the television there is a long window looking out onto a hostile corridor. The new nurse holds up a sign to the window that reads REMEMBER TO STAY HYDRATED. The latest doctor places a hand on her shoulder. The sign falls to the floor. We turn our heads back up to the television. The TV show is starting and we cannot miss a second.

The TV show begins with the usual colourful graphics, animated finger joints and suchlike, accompanied by a smooth voice-over making the announcements. A giant clock—I mean *absolutely huge*—fills the entire screen and a clown's laugh is followed by the catchphrase: "When the clock strikes [SHOW TITLE] it's time for [SHOW TITLE]!" and then the gongs. Minutes and minutes of gongs. So many gongs. But it's those soft and melodious gongs we haven't heard since childhood and so our eyes swell with nostalgia.

The host of the TV show finally breezes in on a wave of adulation at nine minutes and thirteen seconds, lavishly blinking away the biodegradable glitter shower raining upon them. They're wearing the red bustier and matching codpiece again, a favourite amongst us ward dwellers. They pick up this season's megaphone and tell the audience WE CARE ABOUT THE ENVIRONMENT. The audience screeches and we let out gentle whoops as the host twirls in their glitter, the sparkles biodegrading before our nostalgia-swollen eyes. I waggle the most useless parts of my body and the four others perform similar gestures with the disease-riddled parts of their own bodies. This is just a way we can demonstrate our arousal.

The screen fills with an army of assistants that the host of the TV show needs to fasten their 600lb wig in place. We're loath to admit it but it is quite dull to watch this part—the various wooden props and wires and string that are necessary to wrangle it into place are made of such ugly materials, utterly incongruous with the rest of the aesthetic—so that we become absolutely sickened, often to the point of vomiting up our fish and custard. The TV executives must know this because lately, in what can only be described as a desperate scramble for ratings, they have begun plucking out members of the studio audience with oversized mechanical tongs and filming them flailing before setting them down to scurry off as the wig is leveraged into place. The whole segment lasts for around fifteen minutes and nine seconds and given the lack of any real action we use this time to talk to one another, although it is true that we have nothing to say.

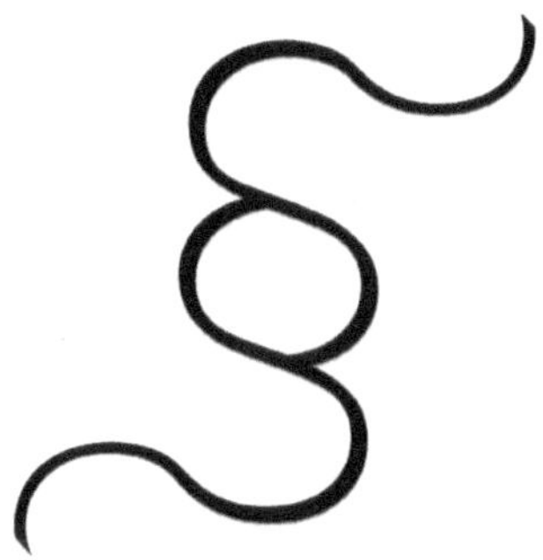

Victoria Manifold's 'The TV Show'
is available in its entirety at
ThisIsSplice.co.uk/2019/07/26/the-tv-show

# About the Authors

DANA DIEHL is a graduate of the Susquehanna University Writers Institute and earned her MFA at Arizona State University. Her début collection of stories, *Our Dreams Might Align*, was published by Splice in 2018. She is also the author of a chapbook, *TV Girls* (2018), and the co-author, with Melissa Goodrich, of the story collection *The Classroom* (2019). Dana lives in the Sonoran Desert of Arizona.

RENEÉ BIBBY is the director of The Writers Studio Tucson, where she teaches advanced, beginner, and teen creative writing workshops. Her work has appeared in *PRISM International*, *Luna Station Quarterly*, *Third Point Press*, *The Worcester Review*, and *Wildness*. Her stories have been nominated for Pushcart Prizes and Best Small Fictions. Reneé is involved in the writing community as a reader at *Atticus Review*, and coordinator of Rejection Competition and Tucson-based Write Wednesday weekly writing meetup.

MICHAEL CONLEY is a writer from Manchester. His poetry has appeared in various literary magazines and has been Highly Commended in the Forward Prize. He has published two pamphlets: *Aquarium* (2014), with Flarestack Poets, and *More Weight* (2017), with Eyewear. His prose work has taken third place in the Bridport Prize and has been shortlisted for the Manchester Fiction Prize. His début collection of stories, *Flare and Falter*, was published by Splice in 2018 and longlisted for the 2019 Edge Hill Story Prize.

ABI HYNES is a drama and fiction writer. Her short stories have been widely published in print and online, including in *Litro*, *Interzone*, and *minor literature[s]*, and she was shortlisted for the Bath Flash Fiction's 'Novella-in-Flash' Award in 2017. Her plays have been performed in venues across the UK. She graduated from Channel 4's 4Screenwriting Course in 2018 and is currently developing original projects for TV.

Thomas Chadwick grew up in Wiltshire and now splits his time between London and Ghent. His stories have been shortlisted for the *White Review* prize, the Galley Beggar prize, the *Ambit* prize, and the Bridport prize. His début story collection, *Above the Fat*, published by Splice, was a Republic of Consciousness Prize 'Book of the Month' selection in April 2019. Thomas is an editor of *Hotel* magazine.

Victoria Manifold is a writer from County Durham. Her work has been published by *The White Review*, *The Chappess*, tNY Press, and Squawkback, among others. She was shortlisted for the *White Review* Short Story Prize in 2016 and 2018. She is the winner of the first BBC Anim8 competition and is currently developing a cartoon with CBBC.

Daniel Davis Wood is based in Birmingham, England. His début novel, *Blood and Bone* (2014), won the Viva La Novella Prize in his native Australia. He is also the author of a monograph, *Frontier Justice in the Novels of James Fenimore Cooper and Cormac McCarthy* (2016), and the novella *Unspeakable* (2017). His second novel, *At the Edge of the Solid World*, will be published by Brio Books in 2020.

# SPLICE

ThisIsSplice.co.uk

www.ingramcontent.com/pod-product-compliance
Lightning Source LLC
Chambersburg PA
CBHW030637190726
48286CB00008B/2561